Bs"D

Dedicatio

I thank Hashem {The Almighty, ... the gift of imagination and
the words with which to express the story that came to mind.
My grandchildren were and are my first audience as I began
the story over many Shabbos visits. I am grateful for their
constant encouragement; it is their confidence and
exuberance that was the catalyst for putting the story to
paper. They are waiting for the next one to be published.

To the very talented illustrator, Marc Moreno; consummate
mentsch and good friend. Thank you!

This December 2019 version moves definitions to the bottom
of the page, for better flow. I thank readers for seeing me
through labor pains of this first book.

Nina Yeret

A woman from another era, country and culture can't rest in peace. We can't and won't know if she's tried to reach others before or employ different methods in her quest, but we are introduced to her as she summons the attention of a young girl- Shana. Her pain and pleas are impossible to ignore, especially with the medium she's chosen. This is a journey this woman directs, to reach out to her dearest. We will encounter herculean emotional and physical efforts to correctly understand and interpret this woman's message; assisted by one person especially, with intuitive and sensitive depth that encourages this journey with gentle direction. She will be the catalyst for her own unfinished story, and lead to another family that needed healing as well.

A MYSTICAL JOURNEY

Many girls hope for excitement in their lives so they can make special entries in their diaries. Everyone in my class has one, I do too but I never really thought anything in my life was that remarkable.

I am the oldest of three children, the only girl. We live in a modest Cleveland neighborhood and are a regular frum family except my parents are Baalei Teshuva. They were raised with the basics but wanted to observe more fully and they bring an appreciation and joy to all parts of Yiddishkeit.

Life was almost predictable, until it totally became fantastic and unnerving. I am writing these words with the permission of my parents and the Rebbe, months after it occurred.

Some details that I would have forgotten I have copied from the notebook and drawings used when I was trying to totally describe and recall the images that appeared to me in my mirror. Yes, other images and yes- a mirror!

Frum {Orthodox religious}

Baalei Teshuva {returnees to observance)

Yiddishkeit {Judaism}

Rebbe {Grand Rabbi}

I am grateful that I had and have the love and support of caring parents and they had the good fortune to trust a truly understanding and great Rabbi. I know that people would come to Him from near and far for their life's issues and children might have found him imposing. Not me! He gave me and us total understanding and guidance and thank you is a small word for what I continue to feel and felt.

The daily schedule of get up- dress, grab the muffin and drink and run to the bus to make it to school on time - day in and day out- would soon become my idea of heaven.

I used to be a girl that wanted to learn, get good grades and was willing to do the homework to achieve this. Chores at home depended on the home work load but Thursday nights, there none assigned and my mother relied on me to help with baths, setting the table for our Friday night Seuda, and organizing the toy area.

People get bored easily until their lives are upended. Then routine becomes what one craves.

We lived with a schedule and relying on what time supper would be and when your parents would be home was always comforting. Until that too wasn't. They noticed much and it was hard to escape their loving and watchful eyes.

I had just celebrated my Bas Mitzva. We had a small celebratory Seuda at home, I received a silver charm bracelet from my parents and per school expectations, I had undertaken a Chesed project. I didn't realize that soon I would need to postpone it because, well- my life changed one day as I was braiding my hair.

Seuda {celebratory or Sabbath meal}

Bas Mitzva {age 12 when girl is responsible to uphold Bible tenets}

Chesed {charitable deed}

I have thick auburn hair and in order to keep it long, it has to be either braided or in a pony (a pony being out of the question for my hair texture).

I was standing and looking into the mirror trying to wrap the ribbon around the length of the braid when I realized I wasn't seeing myself. I blinked thinking perhaps it was a character in a book I was reading. I am an avid reader and "lights out" reminder happens a few times until I actually can put the book down.

But no, this wasn't any person from any book I'd read. This was an old woman, with a brightly printed head scarf and huge brown eyes. O.K. call me crazy but first I thought I was seeing who I'd look like as an old lady, but no way with that clothing! Also, tears were streaming down her face and she was rocking back and forth. I didn't think the old version of me in my mirror would be moving and crying!

My mother's reminder, "Shana, it's getting late," didn't affect the image. She was looking straight at me, seemingly needing something of me. I went to the hall mirror, finished the other braid and raced out to the bus.

The school day was busy and thoughts of the "babushka lady", flew out of my memory. I came home ravenous, as I hadn't eaten breakfast and had also forgotten my lunch; returning to my room to organize my notes and begin homework.

Babushka {head scarf}

I had asked my mother if there was something needing to be done; I am trying to see in what extra way I could help her- this gesture more regularly since I became a Bas Mitzva. She said "Perhaps to help with boys' bedtime later, and if something else came up she'd let me know."

So, to my homework, with a snack until my mother called me down for supper. I helped serve and made sure that Poppa's plate was covered with an inverted plate, as he would come in later to eat.

I would need help with some Meforshiim and as always, the night flew by, unlike the school days which dragged. My brothers, Ari and Moishi were lively and putting them to bed took much longer than anyone would have liked.

My Mother would say Shmah with the boys and would sit with me a little, while I settled into bed, my book under my pillow and then with a kiss on the mezuzah, she'd go downstairs to do the many chores tending to family involves. I couldn't know how much mothers do then; I hope to learn it as a wife and mother when the time is right.

Next day was uneventful so any issues with the mirror were forgotten.

That was Wednesday and today is Friday; short school day and busy afternoon at home. I had washed my hair last night and it needed much brushing and taming.

Meforshiim {scripture commentaries}

Shmah {prayer- Listen O'Israel, said at night}

Mezuzah {scroll encased in holder on doorposts}

I looked at my hair to see if it was braid ready and encountered the lady with the babushka, crying and rocking back and forth.

"No time for this" I thought and I ran to the bathroom mirror to finish my hair-do. The bus was beeping and I had to fly to make it. Fly was a good word because my hair was flying also.

I returned home with a note; my hair needed to be pulled together neatly or it would need to be shorter. School rules. My mother looked at me quizzically and I told her, I'd get up a few minutes earlier from now on. I didn't want my hair cut and I wasn't going to tell her about the lady occupying my mirror, that was making me late.

I know why I didn't share; I thought she would think I was losing my mind or having flights of fancy. My imagination from all the reading sometimes was outrageous and I was working on curbing it.

So, I carried this intrusion myself. I clearly remember this and know I could have spared myself so much fear and anxiety had I confided in my parents immediately. The lady, her sadness and effort to send a message was too overwhelming for a young girl.

Finally- I've been able to connect with a living person. I've been trying for much time that this soul can't quantify; because souls can't tell time. I know I am not at peace. An almanah, my Yaakov lost to me to the reshoiim- may their memories be obliterated as they wanted to obliterate our people and religion. My baby girl, I couldn't care for her in any way or all ways, as I could barely care for myself and I did what I believed was a loving selfless act. I know she would be nurtured, but what would be with my son- my Yaakov? It is this question that torments me and when I am able, I try to send some type of message -somehow / someway to him. He must be grown now and maybe just maybe he will remember the few tefilos that I taught him while his Poppa was away. I didn't know much myself; I used to pray in Yiddish in the Tzenna Rehna or Tehilim, but a boy has to know so much more. I tried to hide him, not letting him go out much at all. Some neighbor must have given "them" our name, for the few zlotys - coins, received as reward. I hadn't prepared him for any danger

Almanah {widow}

Reshoiim {evil people}

Tefilos {prayers}

Tzenna Rehna {abbreviated book in Yiddish for women primarily

Tehilim {Psalms}

He was so innocent and frightened; his little tzizis were ripped off him as he was torn out of my arms but I implored him to remember who he was- He was a Yid (He was a Jew).

So, I try this once more; maybe this young girl will be the right one to help me reach my Yaakov.

Girls are inquisitive and full of energy; so maybe this one will follow through. She seems familiar to me somehow, but I have no time for anything but trying to make her understand the urgency of my message. I hear her, but I know I have no voice. I will have to try other ways to get my message across.

I would like to finally be at peace; knowing that our heritage lives on within both of mine!

Tzizis {religious fringes}

There is no pattern to when the lady will visit my
mirror. I am busy with school. Tu B'Shvat is
almost upon us. My parents set a Shabbos like
table and we partake of different types of new
fruits. My parents like to celebrate with zest so
that we will always carry happy memories and
emulate. My friends like to join; not all parents
invest in each occasion to the fullest, like mine
do.

For example, on the eight days of Chanukah, each
evening is another pre-announced adventure. My
parents who weren't raised exclusively in a Jewish
neighborhood, want us to savor each of our
holidays fully. So, first, no gifts as has become
the current norm- only gelt which had been the
tradition. Each night is either a treasure hunt,
to find the wallets or a play depicting some of
the characters in the Maccabee history. Plans for
our plays keep us busy weeks earlier, raiding the
costume box and making props. Always a different
dessert served and often, my friends join in too.

I was going to sleep a bit earlier so I could get
up earlier and have enough time to both do my
toilette and eat

Tu B'Shvat {holiday celebrating New Year for trees}

Shabbos {Sabbath}

Gelt{money}

Back to Tu B'Shvat though; my mind was on new

Maccabee {Hashmonaiim fought Greek Hellenists to save their
heritage and religion}

Sometimes I would tie up the upstairs bathroom to avoid my own mirror but this wouldn't be a solution or remedy.

Large mirror or small, when the lady appeared, I saw her either more fully or less of her. This time is was the bathroom mirror and I decided to tell her I was Shana, try to get down to the kitchen where I needed to be. I pointed to myself, said "My name is Shana" and this lady shook her head -nodding yes- as if she understood me. No tears this time; so, I thought - o.k. progress. Maybe she wouldn't appear again and maybe if she did, she wouldn't be so sad.

That evening - twice in one day by the way, she reappeared. She was standing near a small table and I was able to see more of the background as well. She was pointing to large pieces of paper - five and each had a letter on it. I could see a "bayz", "lamid", "vov", "mem" and "hay". I sounded out BLUMA adding Hebrew vowels and she shook her head, yes! I pointed to her and asked, "Your name is Bluma?" She nodded and then faded out.

O.K.- she was Bluma and I was Shana and this was weird but less scary.

Hebrew Alphabet depicting b - l - m - h

My mother was calling and I was racing again and my mother gave me a hairband with a shrug. Teenagers it might have meant, I hoped that's what it meant. I wasn't ready to be in trouble for what I couldn't explain and for what was not my fault. I also didn't want a haircut; it had taken three years to get this length after the last serious visit to the hair salon.

I like to doodle and this year, I had wanted to have my notebooks neat and without little drawings. We were again learning Sefer Bereishis, with more Meforshiim, and I wanted to save my notes. If I wanted to teach when I grew up, these could come in handy. That resolve disappeared because I can still see some renditions of the lady and her long skirt and scarf doodled in the margins. I would have forgotten the room- one large room that seemed to be kitchen, eating area, sleeping space and open fire place without the schooltime drawings.

I realize she was from a different era; kerosene lamp and very basic furniture. The fire place had logs stacked near it and a hook with a pot hanging under the top of the fire place.

So, this woman with what looked like peasant European clothes, head covering though, was talking to me through the mirror. Through the ages through the mirror. Wow!

Sefer Bereishis {Book of Bible -Genesis}

Meforshim {commentaries}

While winter days are short, there is a lot of anticipation with Chanukah (already passed) and then Purim plans, which follows a month after the fruit related holiday. Children love this twenty-four-hour Yom Tov, very much, as it involves dress up and sharing of "nosh". My mother involves us in the food plates we would prepare for our friends. In those days all families would bake and slice samples of a few confections and place them on a nice new plate and distribute these. Money was set aside to help the needy; usually the Rabbi would provide names and instructions to help the needy, always though with discretion. My parents liked to go to the market and pay off the "book", anonymously so the families that struggled wouldn't have a huge debt; but also, wouldn't know who had helped them. My mother said it was called "giving quietly to ensure dignity." Sometimes they would give money to be used for Pesach. Other times, they would make an appointment with the shoe store owner and leave money for specific families; the owner would present affordable options as he fit shoes. He was trusted to know to whom and how, so they would feel good with their purchases.

Purim {Holiday celebrating victory over evil Haman)

Yom Tov {holiday}

Pesach {Passover}

Me, I had some babysitting money and I wanted to help one girl in my class whose father had been out of work. I was trying to find a way to help in a kind respectful way and my mother was offering advice. Once a person was hurt, there was no erasing it, so I had to be super careful. Good intentions weren't enough.

With all this activity, I had no trepidation about looking into the mirror. I began making one long braid down my back; less time consuming, more grown up maybe and less time with the mirror.

Bluma however was visiting again; it was Shabbos and I was adjusting the bow on my dress. She was crying again and I saw two candlesticks on the table. She was rocking back and forth and I saw another set of letters; "yud", "ayin", "kuf" and "vayze". I sounded out Yaakov again using Hebrew vowels, and she nodded, tears streaming down her face. She rocked her arms side to side and I tried to ask if it was Yaakov she was rocking in her arms, and she nodded yes. So, I thought I understood, that her baby was Yaakov. I assumed she understood my question as she seemed to have in the last visits.

My father was home and I had to run and I left the room; not sure if she remained or not. I was pale and my parents noticed it.

(Hebrew letters equivalent to y, a, k and v)

Yaakov {Jacob}

They had been asking me tentatively if all was o.k., I wasn't acting like the old Shana. I told them "Everything was fine and yes; I was their Shana." Yeah, their Shana with a mirror friend or visitor or headache. They told me what I knew, if I ever needed anything, big or small, to come to them.

What would I really say? An image in the mirror that wasn't my reflection, a lady from another continent and era most likely was appearing to me, communicating with me. Unbelievable, so I kept it to myself until I could no longer do so.

I remember this without my journal or notebook.
It was Purim day. Of course, I had to make sure
my costume was ready. Our family was dressing as
characters in "The Wizard of Oz" this year. My
friends' parents didn't dress up, but my parents
embraced the holidays always. I was Dorothy –
braids were no problem. My mother had found shiny
red shoes. My mother would be Glinda the good
witch, wand and crown at the ready. My father-
well he wanted to be the scarecrow, overalls and
straw hat and face makeup. Ari would be tin man,
vest and hat and shoes wrapped in silver foil.
Moishi wanted to be the lion and we'd found a
costume that fit him perfectly. I had a basket and
a stuffed dog- Toto for today. We were all
excited and I was making sure that my checkered
blouse was tznius.

Bluma appeared instead and she was "miming" the
shooting of a gun. She had the letters of Yaakov
on the table, she was shaking her head no and kept
shooting the gun. Then she was rocking her arms
back and forth holding a blanket, as if there was
a baby inside. I pointed and asked, "Yaakov?" She
nodded a "No". I didn't get the significance- I
was too overwhelmed by her crying and her trying
to act out shooting and what she wanted to say.
She continued to point to the letters and then
shoot the gun.

Tznius {modest}

I was flabbergasted and frustrated. We had to take Mishloach Monos which we prepared on china plates, out to our friends and neighbors so our day would remain on schedule.

Today was a day we could sample "nosh", each of us would get a plate and with permission place a hammantash or piece of candy or cake on it for "later". Later being when we would return from our holiday deliveries. It was a good system because sampling what was ours, we wouldn't eat it all at once. Mom would wrap up the rest, for another day, marking our names. Efforts to avoid sugar rush.

I ran, saw how my Mother was putting a towel in a box and then resting the plates gently in between paper, and I followed suit. My hands were trembling and I was unusually quiet. My mother told me, "O.K. Shana, tomorrow, we talk. I know something is troubling you." I knew I would try to describe what had been going on- rifles and crying, way too much for me. I'd make them believe it was real and they'd know what to do with this all.

Mishloach Monos {Purim food packages}

Hammantash {three cornered filled pastry-special for Purim}

The rest of Purim was what it is supposed to be; joyous and fun. Our friends loved the way our entire family had dressed up. All in all, with listening to the megillah, the giving of the plates and receiving other packages, the day was great.

Our Seuda was somewhat traditional; my mother liked to keep traditions. We had kreplach and she had made gefilte kraut and she had done

franks in blanks for the boys; wrapped foods represented hidden miracles of Purim. My Challah was a hit! We sang, we ate and then we organized the cleanup. New rule this year, no food upstairs to help begin with Pesach preparation, a labor-intensive process, cleaning out of all food and crumbs from every nook and cranny of the house, primarily though the kitchen and dining areas! Good rule and the boys were old enough to understand and cooperate.

Next day though was discussion day with my parents. Shushan Purim, no school, plenty of time to deal with this.

Seuda {celebratory meal}

Megillah {scroll read on Purim holiday}

Kreplach {like pierogi- meat filled}

Gefilte kraut {stuffed cabbage}

Challah {ceremonial bread}

Shushan Purim {day following Purim}

How could I find the words to describe the sequence of mirror visits to my mother? I was better with the pencil than speaking and I rummaged in the arts and crafts bin for some white or cream construction paper. I sat at my desk into the wee hours and I came up with a few decent depictions of what I'd seen over the last few weeks.

What my mother or parents would see is a woman wearing a long colorful skirt, colorful scarf wrapped around her hair and a background of one room, kerosene lamp on a table and a fire place in the background. I had taken one half of one paper to make what looked like blocks with the letters spelling out Bluma and then drew the same for Yaakov, printing the Hebrew letters carefully. We learn script Hebrew and always write it that way; so, I had to look into my Siddur and copy block/print letters as accurately as I could.

I even attempted sketching a multi- dimensional rendition of this lady holding what seemed to be a baby in a blanket, rocking back and forth. It would have to do- as I am not an artist. I had one of her holding a folded blanket and crying; huge tears on her cheeks. I made an arrow left to right/right to left; to show that she was moving side to side.

Siddur {prayer book}

In another sketch, I drew a rifle, as best as I could; what she'd held seemed to need both hands with a space in between.

I put them in sequential order and finally fell asleep, until my mother knocked on my door to wake me up. She'd wondered how I slept through the boys on morning after Purim sugar rush but she said that Poppa would take the boys out and we would have time to talk. For now: up, davening, breakfast and then the house would be all ours.

As I made my bed, I glanced at my Chumash class notebook; the one I had wanted to be perfectly neat and looked at my drawings to be sure the sketches would tell a story; the story. I didn't even know if I would believe it if someone laid this on me.

My mother is a smart lady; she had a nice plate with grilled cheese and a cup of old- fashioned cocoa for me (my dream breakfast) and her favorite tea for herself and she began the conversation. She reminded me that parents loved their children no matter what and there was obviously something troubling me. There would be "nothing" a child couldn't tell these parents!

Davening{praying}

Chumash {Bible}

I knew that and I told her so. I then told her
that I had drawn some sketches that would help me
lay things out and I went to collect them. I told
her about this lady from another time, appearing
in my mirror for over a month (it seemed like a
life time); and she looked at the drawings and
smiled.

Smiled until she realized this wasn't a story;
this was happening for real and it was affecting
me. She had wanted me to develop this gift of
art; it wasn't something that had interested me.
Now I desperately needed it.

I told her the visits were real and upsetting;
this lady was very sad and trying hard to tell me
something, much more than I could depict from the
room in the background or her hand written letters
or her actions. What I knew was that she was
Bluma, she had someone, most likely a son called
Yaakov but it wasn't clear if he was the child in
the blanket. One time she had nodded yes and when
I tried to clarify, she shook her head- no. I also
couldn't understand where the rifle fit in.

I'd forgotten this but she had put out a loaf of
challah, with pans and a sack of flour and when I
said "Baker", she nodded. Next time I would see
the letters "baize", "ayin", "kof", "kof" and
"raish"-bekker! I had gotten my mother's
attention; she was clearly taking this and me
seriously.

{letters sounding out b - a - k -r /bekker}

She hugged me, said she would discuss this with Poppa and I was to try to go out with some friends and forget about the mirror.

What she did suggest is that she would try to stand outside my room in the mornings, which wouldn't be easy, with all a school morning is with children, schedules etc.   Perhaps she could see for herself and communicate with this lady; one mother to another.

That seemed like a good idea until we realized that the minute someone approached, the lady's image faded. She only visited me!

Poppa processes things intellectually as my mother always says, and when Mom described the situation, he zoned in on the time, the possible venue and the gun. He said he would study up on Jewish history in Europe about a century ago and see what he'd learn. What he did say immediately is that many last names were either descriptions of vocation or the towns in which people resided. Most likely this woman's husband was a baker.

What he later shared was the Cantonist era which was long in its atrocities. "Goyish" soldiers were ordered and given license to oppress Yidden. The Cantonist movement was given tacit support way after the official action ended. Young Jewish boys were targeted; the army would grab them into service at the age of about five or six, for a duration of no less than twenty- five years.

Goyish {Non-Jewish}

 Yidden {Jews}

They'd be taken far away- to Siberia, robbed of
their parents' nurturing and heritage. When they
would be released, they'd be hardened, illiterate
and angry- also irreligious. They would remember
no vestige of religion nor care; it had failed
them seemingly. The wealthier Jews tried to bribe
officers to overlook their children; the majority
of people though were poor and had no means to
either hide their children or leave the country.
Poppa surmised this was Bluma's plight; her pain
was that her Yaakov had been abducted and lost to
her. The fireplace and kerosene lighting would
support the period in history; the rifle, the
scenario of being forced to do something!

Fine, but what to do? Poppa called his Rav and
made a private appointment. His Rav was American
in background and he felt that it would be best to
enlist the aid of the grand Rebbe in Cleveland.
He was originally from Europe and would be more
seasoned and experienced in all facets of
ministering to Jewish people, all ages, types and
stripes, and their issues. This Rebbe might
possess the broader insight to discern a reason
for this particular lady; choosing this young girl
specifically, to try to convey her painful story.

Rav {Rabbi}

Grand Rebbe {Grand Rabbi- higher in religious hierarchy}

Poppa didn't really know of Rebbes, but he called the number and spoke to the Gabbai. He told him he was Yechezkel Levy, he was a simple Jewish man with a beautiful family and an emerging problem that perhaps the Rebbe could direct him on. An appointment was made and my parents engaged a baby sitter for that evening; I would be too wound up to be a responsible sitter.

While I was happy to hand this over to my parents, I hoped the Rebbe wouldn't laugh at a silly girl and think it was imagination or a quest for attention.

The mirror was quiet, since I spoke to my parents and that was fine by me.

Gabbai {Secretary to Rabbi}

The Rebbe's home and shul occupied a larger lot in Cleveland. This address was known near and far to people, all walks of life. Those who had troubles needing advice and guidance lined up. It was also open for those visiting Cleveland. as well. The building was three story; the top attic was the home of Isaac and Sophie, who handled all details in the running of the home and transportation for the Rebbe and Gabbai. The second floor had two wings; one smaller one for the Rebbe and his Rebbetzin separated by a wall and the other wing with large bedrooms and adjoining baths. The first floor had a large prayer room with the Aron Kodesh to accommodate males praying. A smaller room was partitioned for women who came to pray. This set up in keeping with Orthodox rules, separating men and women during prayers and other religious situations. The Rebbe had an office where he met with people. There was a long corridor with comfortable seating for those who waited. There was one room with huge wood table, arm chairs and benches that was where the Rebbe held his "tisch", for Chasidim who would be invited to partake. The kitchen ran most of the rest of the first floor. Additionally, there were two discreetly placed small powder rooms.

Shul {Synagogue}

Rebbetzin {wife of Grand Rabbi}

Aron Kodesh {Cabinet housing Torah-Bible Scrolls}

Tisch {table}

Chasidim {devoted followers}

These details my mother shared when she came home.

Additionally, there was an above the ground basement; but my Mother didn't tell me what uses it had. I imagined a home like this would need much storage and my Mother left it at that. This chit-chat was easier than starting with the conversation and its outcome.

Sophie had worked with the Rebbetzin many years and could anticipate her requests before they were even uttered. She was remarkably efficient and innovative. There were six guest bedrooms and each was painted in another pastel color with towels and linen to match. Each door panel sported the same color so newly arriving guests could look at the foyer small table and take the key ring color coded for available suite (bedroom and small bath). This was the Sophie system! There was one tiny emergency room, used if the house was full. It would be put into use much later in this tale.

Breakfast and dinner buffets were served; sandwiches in lieu of lunch provided upon request. The kitchen was huge and the center of the home, always bustling with activity. Industrial size refrigerator, freezer and stove allowed for cooking in great quantity and freezing ahead of time.

A day worker came to help Sophie with heavy clean up and ever- growing linen that needed laundering.

Isaac would maintain the home (electrical, plumbing and wood repair) as well as shovel leaves, snow and break ice. His domain included the station wagon's upkeep and readiness for any errands the Rebbe required or requested. He also

28

would drive the Rebbe and/or Rebbetzin on their private errands.

The Gabbai would answer the phone calls, arrange private sessions and also meet, greet and "process" the people who brought kvitlech or needed to ask their Shailos.

The downstairs was paneled in dark wood and was regal. Some of the congregants donated their funds and time to upgrade the original home. The Rebbe had a policy though; he wouldn't be told who had contributed; in this way the Rebbe felt he was better equipped to answer questions objectively and treat all equally and fairly. In fact, it was Isaac who took money contributions and made deposits; even the Gabbai was not told, so his treatment of supplicants would also be fair and equal. This was the Rebbe's system!

If the Gabbai felt an incoming call was urgent, it was up to him to consult with the Rebbe and then to rearrange schedules. If a couple was coming, the Rebbetzin would be in attendance as well. Sophie would prepare a tray with tea, sponge or honey cake and lemonade for any children visiting.

Kvitlech {pleas written on small pieces of paper}

Shailos {questions on religious or emotional direction}

All this my Mother shared. She wanted me to picture her experience at speaking to a world renowned Rebbe and his wife, face to face. It was also a way to postpone the conversation about the reason for the visit!

This night, the Gabbai ushered in R'Yechezkel and his wife Iris Levy. The Rebbetzin sat with Iris and R'Yechezkel sat on the other side of the conference table. The Levy's had never had a private meeting with a Rebbe; most of their conversations with their Rav was either in shul or by phone.

The Rebbetzin began speaking and immediately made them feel comfortable. She'd served tea and a slice of cake and asked them in what way the Rebbe could assist?

Mrs. Levy began, describing their oldest child, Shana, recently a Bas Mitzva, and mirror images that had begun appearing about six weeks ago. The woman in the mirror was always the same, from Europe, from another era certainly, living in one room, poor and very pained. She'd spelled out her name Bluma, a last name or profession (or both) Bekker and a name of a son Yaakov; while also rocking a blanket in her arms. A rifle being shot also in some visits. Always crying and begging- only visible to Shana though.

R'Yechezkel continued – saying they'd only become aware of this in the last few days.

R' {prefix meaning Reb- respectful title for men}

He had gone to research a possible period in Jewish history in Europe and what he found that might make sense was the Cantonist era. What they couldn't understand is why reach out to his daughter, such a young girl, after at least a century?

The Rebbe listened and answered that we don't always understand much or fully. He though would like to meet their Shana and summoned the Gabbai to make an appointment for them all, for the next evening. The Rebbe must have felt this was important as it was within the Pesach season with its long list of must do's.

Shana was nervous but her mother had described the set up and the kind eyes of both the Rebbe and Rebbetzin. They spoke in English and were very gentle. Her parents would be with her and all would work out. It would be best if she brought those sketches and her notebook – and whatever else would help organize the details of the conversation.

The Levy family returned the next evening at the appointed time, and were ushered into the Rebbe's office. Again, the Rebbetzin was in attendance and asked that Shana sit near her while she sat near her husband. Her parents thanked the Rebbe for his valuable time and asked Shana to set out the construction paper in the order she'd shown her mother. The notebook was open also, indicating some of the other drawings done during school hours, over the period Bluma appeared to her. What occurred to Shana during this meeting was that Bluma seemed to be able to hear her, but was unable to speak to Shana, and relied on props and the hand-written papers.

The Rebbe listened carefully and asked few questions. One thought was the blanket, was there anything embroidered on the blanket that would be helpful? Shana had seen another color but wasn't able to discern anything remarkable and this was her answer.

Shana had received a lovely bas mitzva gift from her close friends; a wallet type purse with a chain. The flap that closed the purse had a mirror and suddenly the purse and chain began to rattle. Shana was startled but the Rebbetzin told her not to worry. The Rebbe though wanted her to open the flap. Iris and Yechezkel saw a mirror; Shana saw Bluma and the Rebbe and Rebbetzin remained silent. Bluma was there and then Bluma this time very uncharacteristically, slowly faded when she realized Shana was not alone. Clearly Shana was shaken and all could witness how upsetting this was to her!

The Rebbe said he would mull this over and then ask the Gabbai to convey information, over the next day or so. If Bluma returned, in the interim, Shana was to try to write or draw any new details.

The Rebbetzin hugged Shana and told Iris and R'Yechezkel they were really gebenscht to have such a child and they should continue to have Yiddish Nachas from all their children.

The Levy's left and Shana thought - o.k.- I can return to my life. The Rebbe will handle this; isn't that what great leaders do?

Gebenscht {blessed}

Nachas {joy and satisfaction}

The Gabbai saw the Levy family out but he hadn't heard the buzzer, that signaled the Rebbe was ready for the next appointment. The Rebbetzin also hadn't left the room. OK, so he would ask the next in line to wait.

They both sat quietly, absorbing what they'd noticed when the mirror conveyed another image. The Rebbetzin asked her husband whether he had noticed that the blanket being held was a pink type color? He nodded; both realized that it seemed to indicate another child was part of what this Bluma was trying to convey.

The Rebbe asked the Rebbetzin to write down her impressions, as he would- one thought both wrote was that so far, the involved three women's names, were all flowers.

A sound course of action would be to discreetly find out about the Levy backgrounds. The Gabbai was entrusted with this. They were found to be pious people, associated with another shul) and living dedicated Orthodox lives. Shana in Bais Yaakov and two little boys in Yeshiva.

Thinking out loud the Rebbe said he thought it would be a good idea to put an ad in a nationally distributed newspaper that would offer a small reward for information about a Yaakov or Jack- Bekker or Baker between sixty to seventy years old, approximately, with a foreign accent.

Bais Yaakov {Orthodox girl's school}

Yeshiva {boy's institution of learning}

Maybe this family would be interested to do this especially if the mirror continued to flash images.

Clearly this Shana was being upset by the visitations. The Rebbetzin commented to the Rebbe, "A Maaseh Mit a Shpigel", which Sophie overheard as she came to clear the table.

The Rebbetzin retired to her rocking chair in the kitchen to recite some Tehilim. She knew that "why" was never a question expressed; so, dwelling on why a young girl, this young girl and why now after all these years wouldn't help anyone. If this family would need their support, the Rebbe would daven; beseeching Hashem that he be able to do his best to help this girl and family, and perhaps give peace to the old woman in the mirror!

Her husband came from a Rabbinical dynasty; she came from a home of Rabbonim. The pre-war and war years destroyed the fabric of Yiddishkeit in Europe. Millions were taken and the survivors were damaged body and soul, returning to try to rebuild a semblance of pre-Holocaust life. She was beyond grateful to have found a learned and holy person as a husband, with both having survived unspeakable atrocities and loss of some of their children.

A Maaseh mit a Shpigel {an issue with a mirror}

Tehilim {Psalms}

Daven {pray}

Hashem {Almighty}

Rabbonim {Rabbis that interpret Jewish Law}

Yiddishkeit {Judaism}

Not all were that fortunate. All that survived were determined to rebuild and some of the post war unions were less than "tzu-gehpast". The toll of the war didn't always allow harmony or normal function! Theirs had always been a partnership of helping those in need; no judgments and no limits to effort expended, whether by way of tefilos, a shoulder to lean on, dignified assistance or "aitzos" /advice.

The Gabbai was asked to call Mrs. Levy in the morning and suggest that an ad be placed, suggestion of text offered, and that the cost could be covered by Maaser money- as this was possibly a Pidyon Shevuyiim issue; if funds were tight, especially at this time of year. They were not obliged to do so, but it might be a worthwhile effort and shed further light and perhaps bring peace to Shana.

Tsu geh-past {compatible}

Tefilos {prayers}

Maaser {charity-tithe of one tenth}

Pidyon Shevuyiim {redeeming lost or imprisoned people}

35

It was considered a doable idea by both Yechezkel and Iris and an ad using the Rebbe's exact text was arranged and would appear twice in a section called "Lost – Seeking". They decided they would use their telephone number and evening call in hours.

It was close to Pesach, lists of chores in and out of the house to attend to and the possibility that the ad would result in calls was put on the memory back burner. The mirror remained what it should be- a reflection of the person looking into it.

Iris made sure that while the house was readied for Pesach, that the children were involved in the cleaning and organizing in fun ways. Lists- Iris was a big one for organized lists- were made for food items, recipes, clothing alteration or new clothes, new shoes, etc. The house hummed along until the night before Bedikas Chometz; and the kitchen sink and stove would be "kaashered". Counters would be covered with layers of foil and cut to size new vinyl table cloths.

A long- distance call came in- from a R'Berel in Skokie answering the ad placed recently. It had almost been forgotten as the mirror had been unusually quiet and all were Pesach busy.

Bedikas Chometz {search for bread- night before Passover}

Kaashered {rendered Kosher by blow torch or boiling water}

R'Berel said that in the neighborhood next to his, lived a Jack Baker. It seemed from Mr. Baker's neighbor that Jack was ill, in the hospital but he had a European accent and was in the described age range. If there was further direction or interest, R'Berel would be happy to find out more as soon as feasible. R'Yechezkel thanked him for his time and told him the extra inquiry would be welcome, ending the call with the wish for a Chag Kasher V'Sameach. He didn't share reasons for the ad. He himself wasn't sure what anyone would do if they found such a person; as the catalyst for this quest was a woman in a mirror. He knew he would have to be in touch with the Rebbe; one call in reply to the ad.

Very strange, this search, if one really thought about it.

Iris suggested they write a note updating the Rebbe; pre -Pesach was very busy in any household and certainly a Rebbe's home with all the guests and procession of people – in and out - so this was done. A small monetary gift- as a thank you was also enclosed.

Pesach preparations continued and intensified so that the table and Seder plate; were ready to launch another Pesach Seder and excite/enhance their sincere observance of all elements of Pesach.

Chag Kasher V'Sameach {Passover wish, kosher and happy holiday}

Seder Plate {plate with symbols of Passover recitation foods}

Seder {special celebration first two nights of Passover}

Thoughts of anything but the holiday were crowded out.

First day of Chol HaMoed was called game or picnic day in the Levy household, depending on the weather. First the house had to be tidied up and the fridge and pantry replenished. Iris would take the left overs and make a buffet supper because cooking for this Yom Tov was labor intensive for all women and she too needed a break, while also not wasting any usable food.

If the day was nice, they'd pack up matzah sandwiches, macaroons and juice and go to the park. After a cold winter it was nice to soak up sunshine. If the day was inclement, they had new board games to inaugurate on Chol HaMoed, and the parents would play with the children. Most toys that weren't washable were stored away, not to be available on this holiday with its stringent "crumb" rules.

Slow relaxed day; the next day a trip would be planned. Gifts for Afikomen; were already in the house and would be distributed periodically throughout the Holiday.

Chol HaMoed {intermediary days between first two and last two days of Passover}

Yom Tov {holiday}

Matzah {unleavened boards either square or round-specially baked for Passover}

Afikomen {piece of Matzah children take during Seder-bargaining for gift item, before they return it)

That evening - same "call in" hour- R'Berel called once again. He had used a portion of the day to speak to this Jack Baker's neighbor and found out which hospital he was in.

As clergy, he was allowed to visit and he found a paralyzed man lying very still in the hospital bed. Nurse Nancy Davis head of the unit told him that a young woman, Raizel, was at his side all day / every day. She thought it was his granddaughter and there were no other visitors or people responsible for his care and progress. No cards, no flowers, no nothing!

R'Berel continues to relate that he went to the door, knocked softly and introduced himself as a Rabbi coming to visit and see if he could be of any support or help. His wife had made a small bag with macaroons, sponge cake and fruit and he offered this to the young woman, explaining it was Passover, and these were permissible for him to offer as snack foods.

This Raizel was very polite but awkward, she said she'd never met a Rabbi before. He told her anything she needed, he would try to be of assistance and anything she would tell him, would remain in confidence. She shrugged saying there were no secrets; her "Poppa" had been lying like this for quite a few weeks, actually months; and she was hoping her presence would bring him back.

No one was taking care of the home and R'Berel understood that she would come home to empty darkness and surmised that bills would be piling up.

On a first visit it wasn't appropriate to ask any other questions. He decided to go visit the neighbor again and this time Ed was more forthcoming.

Clearly the home was sadly neglected. Weeds were overgrown and the newspapers were piling up. There was an air of emptiness and sadness; windows dirty and screens separating from frames. Ed told Berel that Jack had been weaker this last year and he had had to give up his business, which further saddened him. He'd been without his wife for quite a few years. They had taken over Raizel's care after their daughter had passed on, almost twenty years ago, and it all rested on him until he became ill. Now it rested on Raizel.

R'Berel asked whether perhaps Ed could take in the newspapers and clean the walk-way. Ed was happy to help; he didn't want to crowd Raizel. She was a very private young lady. R'Berel would arrange for a thank you gesture for Ed's cooperation.

Berel left his number and said that as clergy he would try to be of any support – that Ed should call if he thought of something. He also would visit the hospital each Chol HaMoed Pesach day and would bring some food for Raizel and a snack for Nancy, as a thank you.

Yechezkel and Iris thanked him profusely but Berel said this was part of the shlichus.

Chol HaMoed {Intermediate days of holiday}

Shlichus {Rabbinical mission of sect of Chabad Rabbi}

If there was any more clarification from Raizel or hopefully Jack, he'd let them know.

After Pesach, Yechezkel wrote a note to the Rebbe and hand-delivered it to the Gabbai, so the Rebbe would be up to date on this subject.

School would resume, the day after Isru Chag, and that morning, Bluma again appeared in the mirror, so startling Shana. She thought this was over. Bluma was crying, rocking the blanket back and forth. Shana could only think to say "I am sorry- I am sorry" and then ran from the room.

Iris knew the signs; when Shana's braid was uneven and she raced down the stairs and out of the house. She also knew they'd have to either pray this stop or continue to try to find out what this Bluma was trying to communicate.

Isru Chag {day following 8 days of Passover}

The Gabbai had relayed the message and the Rebbe replied by offering a further option, as their daughter was being affected. The Levy's could plan to go to Skokie for a few days and see if anything crystallized. They also could let this go and perhaps the mirror visits would fade over time. If there was no satisfaction, maybe the old woman would give up.

Yechezkel and Iris discussed this; the mirror visits had been insistent and they therefore planned a long weekend trip to Skokie. They'd stay at R'Berel's home and he would take them to meet Raizel, Nancy and Ed; possibly/hopefully, an awake and well Jack. Each of the children would go to a friend so packing a bag for each child plus a thank you gift for each family had to be purchased. Another item for Rifka, R'Berel's wife and this was a small challenge, not knowing this family at all.

It would be three nights and days and they'd collect the children Sunday evening. Iris made sure she had meatballs frozen so she could serve a hot supper Sunday and get the children back on track and to bed at a fairly decent hour for the Monday morning rush.

Map on the seat, Yechezkel drove and they arrived well into Thursday night. They were received with warmth and found a carafe of tea, soda and sandwiches in a sitting room near their bedroom. Next morning the itinerary was to go to the hospital, with some refreshments (supplied considerately by Rifka) and then back to their accommodation.

Shabbos would be peaceful- enjoying R'Berel's shul and his kehillah.

An opportunity to pray with different tunes and customs. Sunday depending on what Friday served up, would be flexible and then back home.

Raizel was surprised at the kindness of strangers but curious how the Levy couple from Cleveland came to visit with her Poppa. Nancy took it at face value; impressed by people's kindness. This young girl had sat for days and weeks on end, with no support or visitors. Each day the toll on her was more evident and she brightened at the thoughtfulness of people. Mrs. Levy asked her gentle questions but she really didn't have many answers. Her Poppa didn't talk much about his life in Europe; neither had her Grandmother. Her parents had died when she was very little and there being no other family, they became her **"onlies"**. She was happy to be cared for and nurtured; she knew some children ended up in the "system". They had legally adopted her and her last name became Baker, to avoid confusion in school and with doctors. She was alright with that as well.

The home was sad- is all Iris could say when she visited with Rifka. A good scrubbing and cutting of weeds could brighten things up. Sagging porch couldn't be easily remedied but some fresh curtains and plants would make it inviting. Always the homemaker but she reminded herself this wasn't her home.

kehillah {congregation}

Iris decided they might visit Raizel again on
Sunday and they also offered to bring her home
from the hospital on Motzei Shabbos. There was
one kosher pizza shop in Skokie and they treated
her to pizza "Melave Malka", not that she knew
what that was. All she knew was this was strictly
dairy- no pepperoni or other options like her
regular pizza preferences.

Rifka had set a festive table and they enjoyed
this treat and Raizel asked a few tentative
questions about what a Rabbi and his wife did when
they came to a place without family and support.
R'Berel and his wife Rivka had moved to Skokie, as
directed by **their** Grand Rabbi-Lubavitcher Rebbe,
to encourage and teach Jewish practice. It seemed
like Raizel's first "window" into understanding
Jewish heritage. She knew she was Jewish but it
wasn't something her Poppa talked about or
emphasized. He stressed honesty, family and
working hard to achieve in life.

During the "Melave Malka pizza meal", a call came
in- long distance, and Shana was crying. She was
by her friend and the mirror in the bathroom
changed so that Bluma was beckoning to her. Once
again with the rifle and then pointing to the
letters spelling out Yaakov.

Melave Malka {meal eaten after Sabbath ends to escort the
Sabbath Queen}

Motzei Shabbos {night when Sabbath ends}

Iris tried to calm her and told her they would change their schedule and come home earlier than originally planned; tomorrow early afternoon. They would leave tomorrow after morning davening and breakfast.

R'Berel and Rifka noticed that Iris was upset and offered help in any way they could. The hospital visit would not materialize on Sunday but they would be in touch once home. Iris and Yechezkel did ask that their best wishes be conveyed to the nurse. A good Rabbi doesn't intrude; so, no further questions were asked.

The Levy's intended to request another meeting with the Rebbe to gain clarity. In the meantime, they took leave of their new Skokie friends and returned to their lives in Cleveland.

Raizel felt bereft; kind new support system leaving as suddenly as they had come but Rifka was kind and she and R'Berel said they'd be in touch. They also would invite Raizel over, when it would work out for her. She told them she didn't like to leave her Poppa until night time's hospital lights dimmed with her Poppa falling asleep. They wondered how she was managing; paying for even the basics of utilities, taxes and food. This they couldn't ask. What Rifka thought she could do was make extra food when she prepared her own family meals and she offered to pick Raizel up some evenings and send her home with hot suppers, or some frozen.

Rifka and her husband knew that they were only messengers; supporting Iris and Yechezkel in this story. In that vein, they could help this sweet Raizel though. They'd be at the ready to help, if

46

feasible, when asked; but, offering had to be done
delicately not to upset the applecart so to speak
and not to be intrusive.

When the Rebbe heard that the image visited Shana even in her friend's home mirror, he understood that the messenger was most persistent and insistent, and that Shana wouldn't easily have respite, if at all.

Again, no one could know why after all these years. Neshamos have their own journeys if this was what this was. He felt a Mamma Bluma was desperate to reach her child and/or children. Observed also was timing; approximate mirror visits at the same time as Jack Baker was hospitalized in critical condition.

He would propose one more plan and it would involve more effort and time by the Levy's. They could embrace the idea or deal with their daughter and maybe, in time, the mirror would be silent. The Rebbe wouldn't become worried; he prayed fervently for guidance, weighed actions and then took all efforts step by step.

A meeting was arranged and this is what the Rebbe suggested. As summer was approaching, perhaps the Levy's could rent a small apartment in Skokie and provide emotional support for Raizel Baker. If nothing else, she'd learn more about what seemed to be her heritage. Best case, Jack Baker would recover and be able to speak with them. Maybe he would mention the Cantonist era and shed light on who this Bluma was, and what she might be trying to say.

Neshamos {souls}

Maybe it wasn't Cantonist; a sad history though seemed to be the catalyst. Understood - though unspoken- was: "The woman in the mirror would NOT be mentioned outside of the Levy and Rebbe's "walls".

R'Berel was again contacted. He said Jack was resting more comfortably. They were doing therapy to keep his muscles from atrophying but he wasn't speaking or seemingly aware. They asked him to look into a small apartment- two bedroom minimum but better three, an amount for rent mentioned and near a Shul. They might spend this summer in Skokie. They would also need a "learning Rebbe" for their two sons- ages 5 and 6 1/2- and inquired about the prevailing cost for this for the summer.

The next week R'Berel called back and said he had this thought, and discussed it with Raizel. Her Poppa's home was empty; no funds incoming for even basic bills or upkeep. It had four bedrooms and was not a huge walk from his shul. She would be amenable to rent it out to them, if she could keep her room. Whatever they were prepared to pay, she'd accept with gratitude.

Rifka had gone into the house with Raizel to assess how to ready this house. It needed a major scrubbing besides koshering of the stove and one sink. The counters would have to be covered and all kitchen items brought in- to support Kashrus.

They would help; it was part of their mission, to set up kosher kitchens.

Kashrus {keeping laws of Kosher}

Yechezkel said they would reply within a day. He and Iris sat down and took out their check book and Maaser (charity) money. If they saved day camp costs for the three children in Cleveland and didn't have extra electricity expenses here at home, there wouldn't be that much extra burden they'd be taking on monetarily. In an emergency, they'd verify if it qualified to be covered by the Maaser (charity) fund.

Yes, they'd have to hire a learning tutor for the boys and yes Iris would be the Morah (teacher) Mommy counselor, responsible for **all recreation**, and yes, Yechezkel would have to drive back and forth for each Shabbos. Either they would see this through to the end or totally shut the door now, mirror visits or no.

They decided to try this one more step, hopefully with resolution. In truth there was no choice. They couldn't be sure the Bluma visits would stop and they worried about Shana since this Bluma came a callin!

Iris had her lists and told Rifka that she would bring all dishes, pots, pans, flatware- all kitchen ware. Another list was food, the majority one of which was pre-cooked, one was games and crafts and the other outdoor activities. Towels of all sorts, linen, pillows, rain gear, toiletries;

Maaser {tithing -charity}

besides kitchen items: slow cooker, Shabbos blech, electric Shabbos urn, besides the kitchen ware, as discussed with Rifka; two sets of all, one for meat and one for dairy, a few for pareve, Seforiim/ siduriim; besides massive cooking ahead of time and MAYBE they could make this happen and still provide a fun summer for the children.

Explanation to the boys wasn't necessary; they were young and they could have fun wherever. Shana saw the sacrifice and realized it was a huge effort to resolve the mirror that was affecting her life. To her friends, it was called a "family summer trip".

Yechezkel's manager was amenable to him taking off Fridays over the summer, rather than the regular week or two he would take in one fell swoop. Shana hadn't realized that she too was sacrificing much; she was giving up the summer with her friends without being able to share the "why", desperately wanting the mirror to stop intruding on her life. Her mother asked her to make a list of ideas that could keep her happy/busy and she did so. Part of each day would be watching Moishi and Ari when her other would go to the hospital and she would earn a bit for this baby-sitting.

Shabbos blech {sheet of aluminum covering flameused to warm pre-cooked food}

Pareve {neutral - contents compatible with either dairy or meat}

Seforiim/Siddurim {holy books - prayer books}

The boys, give them a sprinkler, bikes and sand and they were happy. Coloring books, paint, clay, blocks, puzzles would be packed. "Five and Ten" could allow fresh little prizes if need be, especially during the Nine days where no music or swimming was permitted.

They were given a brocha by the Rebbe for their mesiras nefesh and arrangements were made with Raizel. It was explained to her that kitchen duties would be exclusively handled by Iris, Mr. Levy or Shana- a nice way of saying – kitchen totally off limits to her. She would be served all meals and foods; snacks would be prepared for her as well. It would be "kaashered" and there would be separation of milk and meat/poultry. They apologized but if she wanted to eat out, that food couldn't be brought in while they were renting and residing in the home. They couldn't take a chance on treif mixing with their kosher kitchen/ foods. They would put little notes on light switches or fans, to indicate which couldn't be touched on the Shabbos. This would include a slow cooker and the water urn, used for Shabbos as well.

Nine days {period of mourning in summer}

Brocha {blessing}

Mesiras nefesh {extra devotion}

Kaashered {sink-stove-oven-made kosher}

Treif {non-kosher food}

She agreed but said she could contribute to the maintenance of the home by helping with the laundry. She was so relieved a few dollars would be coming in. The bills had piled up. She'd also be happy with the array of tasty foods Iris was known for.

Iris traveled with Shana ahead of time, bringing the first load of vital items and to begin preparations. Yechezkel rented a U-Haul and brought the boys, play equipment and countless boxes and bags. They all worked the first two days to set up a kitchen that could be used reliably. Labels for what would be dairy and meat sections of the counter, as well as drawers were affixed. The pots/pans, dishes and flatware belonging to Jack were boxed, labeled and put in storage for the summer. After the kitchen was tackled, bathrooms and windows were next. Mattresses were vacuumed and aired and the beds made with Levy linen. The rest of the basics could and would be done more slowly.

Raizel brightened when she saw what a good scrubbing and new curtains did to bring the home of her youth to life. When she was younger, her Grandmother baked and sewed and there were plants on the sills and in the garden.

Being able to open windows that glistened encouraged her to go further and resume work on the garden, pruning and planting. Shana was happy to join Raizel and they began slowly bonding over time. The boys liked digging also and were good at pulling the weeds out. A good plan all in all!

All fell into a schedule. Friday Yechezkel would arrive with a list of frozen items that Iris had designated for the week. The kitchen smelled like Shabbos; cholent bubbling; no matter that it was hot and humid outside. Potato or noodle kugel, gefilte fish – some type of cake and roasted chicken were the delicacies that graced their Shabbos table. Rifka made sure to help Iris with shopping for fresh Cholov Yisroel dairy items and fresh produce. White cloth on the table with challah cover, wine cup and some divrei Torah, courtesy of R'Berel.

Raizel was always invited to partake. The first Friday night she sat down, she realized they were wearing special clothing; not the regular day and play clothes. The next week, she came in with a white blouse and dark skirt and this was her first effort towards honoring Shabbos.

When the schedule worked it whistled. When it didn't, Iris had to think quickly on her feet because she was wife, mother, camp mother and woman trying to connect with this motherless girl and sick grandfather.

Cholent {Sabbath stew cooks overnight- meat-potato-beans}

Kugel {pudding}

Cholov Yisroel {certified Kosher dairy}

Divrei Torah {Bible portion commentary}

Yechezkel was miles away and Iris only asked Rifka
for support, if no other solution could be found.
This was their mission and she didn't feel
comfortable disturbing Rifka's routine, more than
they already had. She knew R'Berel and Rifka
cared for quite a few families in Skokie, not just
Levy's.

The first three weeks of the Skokie summer went pretty much according to Iris's plans. Wednesday night was the regular "Iris and Yechezkel call night" unless there was an emergency. Iris would tell her husband, which food packets to bring for this week's Shabbos and they would catch up; about the boys' learning, activities and anything mirror related. He was in charge of making sure he rented a sturdy car; they had worked out a three-month rental agreement because Iris would need their station wagon in Skokie. Three months to cover first load of items out there to clean up/set up and committed three- month rental of the home, to leave a little extra rent money for Raizel, at the end of the summer.

He'd arrive early Friday morning and then after a brief nap, he would join R'Berel and visit with Jack Baker. They'd speak to Nurse Nancy and to the physical therapist Alex assigned primarily to Jack's care while also offering Raizel a little respite from sitting there for hours.

Iris had offered to teach Raizel and Shana crocheting and Raizel took to it quickly. It gave her hands something to do, those long days besides being comforted by the rhythm of the craft.

Friday was the only weekday that Iris didn't go visit; she was busy entertaining the children and preparing Shabbos in a kitchen which wasn't hers and still unfamiliar. Everything took more time and the house always got a once over L'Chvod Shabbos.

L'Chvod Shabbos {in honor of the Sabbath}.

Week four though, the weather changed. What had been dry and warm weather erupted into thunder and lightning a good portion of the week. Outdoor play wouldn't work and Iris had to be creative in keeping active little boys busy. She decided they would make a chocolate babka - and leave an extra cake packet in the freezer at home, maybe for their first week back. She sold the project plus clean up after, by offering them all fresh babka with chocolate milk as a reward. This would have been a good solution except the learning Rebbe couldn't tutor that day either. One long summer day stuck indoors; what to do.

Iris wanted to go to the hospital and she bribed the boys- with big nosh bags and coloring. They had to remain in the waiting area and they had to sit still with Shana. One half hour, that was all. She'd go, bring Raizel a snack, touch base and see if there were any changes. Shana would be coming as well; it would be her first time.

Raizel had invited her to stop by several times but Shana always made excuses; she was frightened.

Iris told Shana she could sit in the solarium with the boys or maybe be with Raizel for a short while and she'd be with the boys; up to her.

They arrived and ran into the hospital. Nancy had given the family passes and Iris settled the boys down on the chairs. Near the solarium was a huge therapy room. The boys watched a man in a white jacket wheeling another man into the room and settling him close to a table. They were curious and left the chairs to stand by the double door. The man had taken out what looked like play dough-clay and was talking to the man, sort of belted

into the wheel chair. Moishi and Ari didn't know
that this man was in fact Jack Baker – the first
time for his physical therapy outside of his room.
They were just curious and liked clay.

The therapist was Alex and he saw two cute little
boys watching, and waved. That was all the
invitation they needed. They ran over- Ari on one
side of Jack and Moishi on the other. They saw
clay sitting and Jack sitting. They did what made
sense to them; each took one of Jack's hands to
teach him what to do with the clay. They rolled
it back and forth and Alex stood by smiling; it
was good enough progress. A faint change in
Jack's lips that qualified as a crooked smile, was
an additional reward.

Nurse Nancy making her rounds was ready to tell
the boys- "Outside was their place," but Alex
nodded, she observed and then made notes on Jack
Baker's chart.

Shana had been sitting on the other side of the
solarium, watching from a distance, realizing the
boys weren't in their spots and she went to find
the boys. She wasn't yet ready to see this Jack
Baker- fearful of the unknown. She knew she was
disappointing Raizel – maybe even her mother- but
she couldn't force herself. It had to come from
her naturally, if it came. Her mother was putting
no pressure on her, in this matter!

Iris ended today's visit and went to collect the
boys. Nancy told her that they'd been very useful
and they could return any day- it seemed Jack
responded well to them.

They waited until Jack's hands were cleaned and he was returned to his room. The slightest activity tired him and he immediately went to sleep.

Iris figured today was working itself out; thunder or no and she'd take it one day at a time. Hashem would always help her; certainly, when she was trying so very hard to help others.

Hashem {Almighty}

Iris now had less anxiety; the boys could perhaps could be welcome and possibly useful if she had to include them in her daily visit to the hospital. There was talk of Jack Baker being transferred to another wing of the hospital, for more intensive rehabilitation. If that were the case, they wouldn't have Nurse Nancy's more welcoming, lenient and understanding reception of people, and children, who weren't relatives, visiting daily.

One day at a time; always worked the best especially here in this Skokie summer; this was the mantra she kept repeating.

The next few days reverted back to schedule. Shana was a big help keeping the boys occupied and also helping keep the house up. One could relax standards with one's own house, but here they were tenants. Iris also wanted to leave the place with enhancements so that Raizel could benefit afterward as well.

Iris counted down each summer week this year; grateful that the plans could work and hopefully some good, result from the effort. Wasn't easy for the family to be separated like this.   Shana was missing her friends and in truth so was Iris. All were missing Yechezkel. So hopefully there would be clarity and resolution. So far there had been no Bluma appearances in this Skokie home; that made all the difference!

This week again needed ingenuity. Iris took the boys along with her and Shana. The incentive for excellent behavior was to buy them roller skates, for good behavior. It was something they'd wanted and which she had postponed. It would mean hours outside until they mastered balance and she would

have liked Yechezkel to teach the boys! Iris
wanted Shana to make a visit into the room even
for a brief moment, but it would have to be up to
Shana; no incentives for her because she wasn't a
baby anymore. She would either overcome her fear
and reservation or she wouldn't.

Alex saw the boys and included them in Jack's
visit to Rehab. Jack actually seemed to remember
them and they took their places and helped move
his hands with the clay. They would be given
chunks for themselves, to take home. Nancy was
encouraged, with Jack's response and slight change
in ability; but made sure that Jack wouldn't
overdo it.

Iris was in with Raizel, having brought a thermos
with coffee and some rogola pastry. These were a
favorite of Nancy's as well and there was a baggie
with a sampling for her too.

Shana came to the door, knocked slightly and came
in. She apologized to Raizel for taking so long
to visit. Raizel told her she understood; she had
always been afraid of hospitals but here she had
no choice. Poppa needed her.

Shana had learned that one should say a Kapitul of
Tehilim when one visits a Choleh.

Rogola {mini pastry}

Kapitul Tehilim {paragraph of Psalms}

Choleh {one who is sick}

She went to the foot of his bed, and would have begun reciting the verse she knew by heart, but her purse, the one with the mirror inserted in the flap, began shaking and moving. As she was standing still, this was very odd.

Suddenly the following words erupted loudly from Shana- **"Yaakov ben Bluma- Gedenk di bist a Yid"**. After uttering these words in a foreign tongue, she began crying. Words coming out of her mouth in a language and voice that were not hers; scary! Jack Baker stared at this young girl, a tear forming at the corner of each eye and said **"Modeh Ani"**.

Raizel was flabbergasted; here she'd been sitting for weeks, no months, on end and no word from her Poppa- to her! Now his first utterings were in a language she didn't recognize, to a stranger to him. And truthfully, what happened to Shana?

Iris ran to find Nancy so she missed her Shana again repeating "Yaakov- Gedenk di bist a Yid" and Jack Baker trying to lift his hand seemingly toward his eyes and saying **"Shmah Yisroel"**.

Nancy heard the tail end of this and sternly asked Shana to please leave. Shana shaking turned to her Mother, who told her all would be alright.

Yaakov ben Bluma- Gedenk di bist a Yid {Yaakov son of Bluma, remember you are a Jew}

Modeh Ani {first morning prayer- I thank Almighty}

Shmah Yisroel {Hear O'Israel-prayers said morning and night}

Shana was more than o.k., with leaving this room. She'd feared coming and she hadn't at all been wrong.   Raizel looked puzzled and Iris told her she'd explain the words a bit later.

Nancy checked pulse and blood pressure and cleared the room from all except Raizel; no more visitors today.

Iris collected the boys who were munching on potato chips and soda (bribery foods) and set out to find a store that sold good skates. She would call Yechezkel tonight after he returned from work; it seemed important that he get a timely message into the Rebbe.

Shana's purse had stilled as suddenly as it began shaking and Shana threw it into the station wagon; most likely she'd put it away and not use this particular gift anymore. Some gift- more like a headache! There were no good words to comfort Shana despite Iris's huge effort; this mirror-any mirror, was unpredictable in the tumult it created.

That evening Iris waited for Raizel and explained to her the few foreign words but **nothing** about the purse or anything mirror related. Possibly when one is recovering from a stroke, they draw on memories of their first language. This is what Iris surmised and offered as a plausible explanation. Shana's role, also was left as a mystery.

Iris would wait to hear how Yechezkel's conversation with the Rebbe would affect and direct their time here.

Iris speaks to Yechezkel and tells him to call her back, no matter the time, if there's any update from the Rebbe.

The Gabbai had taken his call and Yechezkel had run over for a very late appointment with the Rebbe. He had written down what had transpired with Shana, the mirror purse shaking and what Jack Baker had said. These had been his first words since his stroke; they were clearly enunciated and emotional and certainly not in English.

The Rebbe told Yechezkel that his wife and children should continue with the routine. If there were any other changes, to promptly advise the Gabbai. The Gabbai would be in touch tomorrow with a possible update as the Rebbe wanted to let thoughts come to him overnight. When the Rebbe decided and confirmed his plans, Yechezkel would be told the Rebbe and wife would be visiting Skokie.

In fact, the Rebbe asked the Gabbai to clear the schedule for the next ten days. The Rebbe and Rebbetzin would be going away. The Gabbai said he too would make arrangements to leave and the Rebbe said- "No, for this trip I will need Isaac and Sophie." The Gabbai hid his dismay and hurt; it was he that always traveled with the Rebbe.

The Rebbe however sensed his emotions and said, "I need you here and I believe they need to be in Skokie with me."

The Shamash was grateful for his Rebbe's sensitivity and words of encouragement. He had been serving this Rabbi for decades; first in Europe and then re-establishing a center for Chassidius, in America, culminating in the Cleveland shul. In fact, he had first served the previous Rebbe. He had seen this Rebbe sense and intuit lofty thoughts and put in motion, tefilos, and almost miraculous resolutions and brochos for myriad seemingly impossible situations. He prepared an envelope with emergency funds, if needed. He also would speak to Isaac, about how to schedule hours and intervals for any people seeking the Rebbe's advice while in Skokie, and how to best prioritize and maximize time.

Sophie would also leave detailed instructions for the day worker about schedule and priorities, so the household would run. The Rebbetzin's friend would cover the kitchen meals, albeit a bit more simply and Sophie labeled foods to be used during their time away. The guests here still needed to be cared for.

Shamash {another word for secretary to Grand Rabbi}

Chassidus {devoted followers of Grand Rabbi}

Tefilos {prayers}

Brochos {blessings}

In the meantime, R'Berel would help find accommodation for the Rebbe and this would allow the Rebbe a few hours daily to meet some of the neighboring Yidden who would hear about his sojourn and wish to meet this great personality.

A trip such as this, made by an elderly and revered Rabbi, of a Rabbinical dynasty, heightened the significance of why the Levy's initiated their search for a Yaakov or Jack Bekker or Baker and why they turned their lives upside down the way they had.

The Rebbe and Rebbetzin arrived and their first conversation was to include R'Berel somewhat more, in the sensitive and confidential reasons for the Skokie visits.

R'Yechezkel would take off a few days extra that would coincide with the Rebbe's arrival. Nurse Nancy would be advised that a grand Rabbi would be visiting the hospital to speak with Jack Baker, and it might be a conversation with sensitive content.

This Rebbe was world renowned; coming suddenly to a small community such as Skokie was a huge deal and R'Berel was honored to be able to assist in this visit.

As it happened, there was an apartment down the block; the family would be going to the Catskill mountains in upstate New York for a few weeks and R'Berel and his wife made all the necessary arrangements for the Rebbe's entourage.

Yidden {Jews}

That family was honored to have a person of this stature stay in their home. Rifka arranged to have it aired, freshened up and to stock the refrigerator with dairy, produce, drinks and juices.

Sophie was helping the Rebbetzin cook and freeze so that their meals away would be taken care of also. The "samovar" for tea – a must! The Rebbe's Bigdei Shabbos and the Seforiim and seduriim, the Rebbe preferred were also prepared for the trip. R'Berel would provide the Sifrei Torah needed for Shabbos prayers in the guest house as well as folding tables and chairs.

Isaac prepared the station wagon for a long drive, got a map and wondered why this time, it was he and his wife that were accompanying this very holy couple. No questions though. This is what the Rebbe said, and clearly the Rebbetzin was very on board with this arrangement.

In Cleveland, the Gabbai would man the fort; handle the incoming phone calls, re-schedule appointments and if there was something that was deemed an emergency, he would either call R'Berel or Iris Levy, to reach the Rebbe.

Bigdei Shabbos {special clothes for Sabbath}

Seforiim / siddurim {holy books and prayer books}

Sifrei Torah {holy Bible scrolls}

Iris was told the Rebbe and entourage would be
coming and she planned to bake a welcome cake and
buy flowers for their time in Skokie. She'd
noticed the Rebbetzin serve sponge cake, so she
hoped hers would not flop. Yechezkel knew not more
than they were being joined by this great Rebbe,
seemingly in reference to the purse mirror, Shana
and Jack Baker.

First day had been travel and rest day; the second
day R'Berel would take the Rebbe and Rebbetzin to
the hospital. Nancy had been told ahead of time
that the Grand Rabbi was coming to visit with Jack
Baker and offer spiritual support; and she was
duly impressed. She'd never seen such care for an
anonymous stranger as she was witnessing now. The
staff and she would monitor Jack more closely;
they didn't want him under too much stress. It
could bring adverse reactions.

She'd never met a Grand Rabbi so when he arrived
with his wife and the other couple, she tried to
be extremely respectful, as she would treat her
own spiritual mentor. She was rewarded with a
kind smile and a gracious thank you for her care
of Jack Baker and his Raizel.

Iris knew of this visit and she made sure that
Shana would watch the boys for a longer time
today. Always with a bag of refreshment for
Raizel and a treat for Nancy, Iris also packed the
thermos with tea and lemon along with cake slices
for the Rebbe and entourage.

Raizel couldn't believe how many cared so deeply
about her family's plight. She and Poppa had been
"it" for so very long. When he took ill, she had
been devastated. He was her rock and last living

relative; he had to be o.k. She might just fight her fear and try to ask Iris some questions. The truth might be easier than what her vivid imagination was drawing.

This grand Rabbi's arrival would be the Levy's almost seventh week in her home. She'd wait and see, which is essentially what she had been doing since mid-January when her Poppa had collapsed. So far R'Berel was very gentle and understanding; R'Yechezkel also, and she hoped that this great Rabbi would be supportive and comforting as well. This is how she pictured a great religious leader would be.

There was more tension for Iris especially this upcoming week; the fragile summer routine would be changing and needed much juggling. Time was precious and much needed to be clarified. Keeping Ari and Moishi occupied while the Rebbe was in town would be a challenge. Whenever she was preoccupied, they would invariably act out. She didn't need that now! Shana needed extra t.l.c.- she had been rattled by the words that came out of her mouth, Yaakov's response (she was certain he was Yaakov) and Nurse Nancy's recriminations and edicts. Iris didn't know where to put herself first. She too wanted to see and hear events, first hand.

If she wasn't successful in calming her own daughter, she'd ask Yechezkel to ask the Rebbetzin and Rebbe to try to put things into perspective for her. Iris shouldn't have worried- at least about the boys. Isaac and Sophie were wonderful with children and they happily filled in, when Iris and Yechezkel were otherwise engaged. The little house enjoyed their touches as well. Windows opened more easily, and home- made vegetable soup greeted the exhausted adults. This was their art; anticipating needs and providing quiet comfort and support. They'd been with the Rebbe even in Europe, following him from city to city. Cleveland it seemed, would be the last "home" and this was a short -home away from home. Whatever the Rebbe and his Rebbetzin needed!

The Rebbe and Rebbetzin met with Shana after settling in, to get a firsthand "picture" but also to reassure her. She laughed to herself about her worries about meeting them again, after the episode in Jack's hospital room. He and his wife

were so gentle and understanding. They heard her
out and then told her that she'd done nothing
wrong! She had been frightened; not able to
dismiss her only visit to Yaakov Baker. Gentle
conversation put her at ease. The Rebbe told her
that "We" didn't always know why things happen;
but we need to always try our best - as it
presented itself." In this case, much effort and
time had been spent to find a son of a woman long
gone, seemingly not at peace. It brought them all
to Skokie, to a hospital room and a sick man and
granddaughter.

The Rebbe at some point would need Shana to be in
the room when He would visit, and her parents
would be there with her. If it became too "much",
He would motion to her mother to escort her out.
The challenge here was that Yaakov was ill and
couldn't speak at all; besides the few words
uttered from his childhood memory. He hadn't
talked about his past much with his granddaughter,
but they would take this slowly. The Rebbe
realized no one knew for a certainty about
Yaakov's wife / daughter and her husband; details
which would determine if Raizel was even a Yiddish
kint; except for something Raizel had said. Her
Poppa told her to remember she was a Jew.

Did this Jack Baker know the halacha (Jewish law);
the mother had to be Jewish in order to confer
that status on the child?

Yiddish kint {Jewish by birth based on maternal bloodline}

The Rebbetzin had a very welcoming heart and gentle touch; this would be her area to try to unravel. Raizel certainly would feel more comfortable speaking to a mother figure.

The time was upon them. The Rebbe and his wife; Levy couple and Shana came to the nurse's station and Nancy took them all into the room, except for Shana. Nancy gently told her she'd come and get her if Jack seemed calm and that she was sure Shana didn't and wouldn't do anything deliberately to hurt the patient. She was sorry if she had been abrupt that last time; her patient's needs had to come first.

Raizel sat quietly in her chair and the Rebbe sat in another chair brought in for him, directly across from the patient, looking at Yaakov. First, he recited some Psalms for the Choleh (sick person). He then spoke in Yiddish in a soft melodious voice; beginning by introducing himself as a Rabbi originally from Europe, descendant of Rebbes. He continued softly, still in Yiddish as he saw that this Yaakov was "following his words"; talking about the war and wars which destroyed much of Yiddishkeit there and that many refugees came to America. Religious guidance was needed in various cities and he was a Rabbi now in Cleveland, Ohio.

Families had been destroyed and broken; Torah learning disrupted and each Rabbi was committed to healing and restoring Jewish life and observance.

Halacha {Jewish law}

Yiddishkeit {practice of Judaism}

So many wars, so many times, Yidden had to rebuild totally. He touched upon brutal pogroms; and gently mentioned the era of Cantonist destruction of families and boys growing in their Yiddishkeit. The Rebbe paused with this, letting Yaakov digest the message and the specific word- Cantonist. Known in history that even after this decree officially ended; it continued for decades without legal recourse and protection to the families. The Rebbe tried to see if there was any specific reaction to either type of atrocity, pogrom or Cantonist. It would seem "Cantonist" resonated and reasonably confirmed that Yaakov was one of its victims!

Yaakov was understanding all spoken in Yiddish but with mention of Cantonist, Yaakov began to cry. The Rebbe waited briefly and then continued, even more gently now, describing how he had become involved - it seemed a Yiddishe Mamme (Jewish mother) couldn't rest in Gan Eden - she was trying to send a message or messages to her son and possibly family, in a very unusual fashion. Yechezkel was able to follow some of what was spoken; Iris and Shana not at all and the Rebbetzin motioned that she would explain all later.

Torah {Bible}

Gan Eden {Heaven- literally Garden of Eden}

Jack Baker listened intently; tears flowed down his cheeks. His Mamme – he remembered her loving warmth and her many tears. His father had had to serve in the secular army and was far away. Young boys were being snatched and ripped away from

their homes. He had only learned this when he joined hundreds like him, stolen away. He remembered their hut, one large room and a loft and the comfort she provided within those walls. She tried to hide him or find a safe family to take him; all efforts to no avail. The only thing she could do is keep reinforcing that he must remember – "He was a Yid". He forgot all of the rituals he'd learned in his short six years; or maybe they were just buried under fear and pain., But this he never forgot; **"Gedenk die bist a Yid."** The exact words that girl had spoken the other day, sounding exactly like his Mamme. Unbelievable!

The Rebbe had been quiet, watching Yaakov's face as if he could see his thoughts. He then continued his narrative. "A young girl- Shana- saw a lady in her mirror, quite a few times. A woman with large brown eyes, crying and begging for her son- whose name was Yaakov. The Rebbe briefly described the details as they were elicited- the room, the mode of dress, baking paraphernalia which might also mean a last name- and trying to depict shooting while also cuddling a blanket, to imply a baby. Bluma Bekker bereft and alone."

Yid {Jew}

Jack sobbed as he remembered. Nancy stood at the ready but the Rebbe gently put his hand up to wait. "The tears are healing tears- therapeutic!"

Jack / Yaakov silently processes the words this Rabbi is uttering: yes, this was his mother. She wasn't alive; he'd been told this when he returned after his thirty (30) years of servitude. His dream -all those first cold frightening years as a child – was to return to his Mamme. Not to be! No father, he believed he had died first; now no mother and no home. Gentiles now lived in what had been their hut. He had become angry and bitter. The neighborhood was demolished; no vestige of friends or neighbors- cheder or shul. He was going to work to earn money, get papers and leave this oppressive hateful town and country. It took time, more years than he had anticipated. He had returned to his home one evening before he left, late at night, shovel in hand. From his family "secret spot", he pulled out a small leather-bound book wrapped in paper. If it was still here it meant that he should believe and accept that his Mamme was no longer alive. She wouldn't leave without this book. His legacy, slightly warped and moldy, but that had been his life too!

After about fifteen years, he lost count, he ended up in the mid-west of the United States.

He'd met a Jewish woman, married her and they'd had a daughter- Lily. Too painful to use his mother's name Bluma and chose a name of another beautiful flower, to honor his mother.

Cheder/shul {boy's school - synagogue}

He was hardened and very sad. He worked hard, in a bakery, amazingly. He began as a shlepper, heavy sacks of flour and ingredients and up nights kneading the voluminous mounds of dough. Slowly, he learned the trade and then bought the retiring owner out. Long hours providing bread and rolls during American war years but it allowed him to buy a small home and raise the love of his life- Lily.

He had only touched the leather book a few times, to record vital information. Otherwise, too much pain that he could ill afford to confront.

As Jack remained with his memories, the Rebbe says he will Im Yertza Hashem; return soon, and then he and entourage quietly leave. It seemed more likely this was the right Yaakov, but the Rebbe would use his time here to try be more certain. Shana was totally relieved.

The Rebbetzin thanked the nurse and left a box of cheese kuchen (cookies) for her. They would return tomorrow or day after.

Im Yertza Hashem {G-d Willing}

Raizel sat quietly, holding her Poppa's hand after the room emptied. He was somewhere else. Quiet, not angry, not sad, even with his tears, but definitely not here in the room. She knew he had had much pain in his life. Her peers had uncles, aunts, cousins and friends to share parts of life. She and her Poppa had a very empty existence, certainly after Momma had passed on. Pictures of Raizel's mother remained in the album. She early on realized any question she'd broach would cause painful silences and tears. Best to be happy with what she had. They had tried to make sure she fit in, with her public-school classmates. She really didn't though because they all had young parents. Her beloved grand parents weren't young and seemed weighed down with burden and pain. Her Poppa was not at all well versed in American "ways".

Raizel suddenly realized both she and her Poppa were both traveling, outside of these walls, in their thoughts.

At the end of the day, Raizel returned home to a large meal taking place. She changed into the skirt and blouse she had bought to honor "Shabbos" with the Levy's and joined all. She was quietly asked if she cared to bring out any albums or pictures of her, as she was growing up. The Rebbetzin told her, she could share as little or as much as would be comfortable for her.

The album was easy enough. Old black and white photos, with some written captions and descriptions showed a younger Poppa, with his wife, in their apartment. Many pictures of Lily as a toddler, teenager, graduating from high school and then in a bridal gown. Lily expecting and then holding, new born Raizel. Raizel's finger would caress this photo. The pictures stopped when Raizel was about three and this album held no more pictures. The next one showed Raizel, in school, baking with her Momma and a few with a very taciturn Jack. No clue to shul affiliation or if either wedding was conducted according to Halacha, in either album. The question – was Lily's mother authentically Jewish would have to be broached if they were to handle all elements of this quest, correctly.

It had been a long day and the Rebbe and his wife returned to their accommodation with Isaac and Sophie. Shana and Raizel quietly washed and dried the dishes and no plans were announced for the next day.

Raizel didn't go upstairs as she normally would have; she waited for Iris- she had things on her mind. All things that seemed extraordinary; strange people visiting her Poppa, undue interest in his care and even the renting of the house, she had taken at face value. Now though she couldn't dismiss things that didn't make sense. The episode when her Poppa uttered words in a foreign language, and called for his Mamme, like a child would, clearly wouldn't allow her to accept without questions; who were they and why were they here?

Halacha {Jewish law}

Why would a great Rabbi travel to visit a stranger- her Poppa? Why would he speak another language to her Poppa with the assumption that Poppa would even understand any of the words? What made her Poppa suddenly able to both understand and respond, when she'd been sitting weeks on end, prattling along with not a yes, no, blink or smile? He'd never mentioned knowing Yiddish and yet he clearly had followed every word this Rebbe had spoken. She'd never heard him utter anything but English, albeit accented!

Raizel was also troubled by the emptiness she would face, when the summer ended. This she wouldn't discuss; no one owed her anything. Poppa would want her to be grateful for blessings she had and maintain dignity. Nancy though understood her fears and feelings and said she'd remain by her side, always- no matter what!

Iris wasn't prepared for these questions, she should have expected them but when they didn't happen immediately, she thought they wouldn't. She prepared a fortifying cup of coffee and gently began telling Raizel that some of the tenets of living an Orthodox Torah life was "Chesed" and even sometimes but not often one called, "Pidyon Shevuyiim. In this case it would seem that a mother was grieving for her child that might have become lost to her. They couldn't ignore the mother, the repeated incomplete messages, nor the opportunity to help people in need.

Chesed {care and involvement}

Pidyon Shevuyiim {recovering lost people}

Of course, Raizel then questioned which mother and what plea and how could it have been transmitted so long ago to be acted upon decades later. This explanation however was not feasible for Iris to include now because of the exact method Mother Bluma employed. Iris wasn't equipped to know how much or little to share; no one had thought to ask the Rebbe how to speak with Raizel, and what to say, when and how. Now she was face to face with legitimate questions, and wrong untimely answers might do damage. Iris herself wasn't even sure if they were on the right track; even though with the Rebbe's visit, it seemed to indicate -yes.

She answered the question with the truth- "I will ask the Rabbi, just as we have been all along. It may seem like an immature or foreign concept but Orthodox Jews, observant Jews usually have a "Moreh Derech", to decide pivotal and crucial questions that arise. We've not done any one thing in this summer journey without guidance and his blessing."

Raizel would have to be content with this. It was the absolute truth.

Raizel sensed the truth behind the words, despite it being a foreign concept to her. Once she was seemingly calm and went up to bed, Iris sent a message to the Rebbe that Iris herself would need some time and that Raizel too would need attention; she was asking many questions. The visits and all the focus in fact concerned her only relative in this world and that affected her.

Moreh Derech {spiritual adviser}

Yechezkel had been learning Talmud in the dining room and he thought she had handled the questions perfectly. Now to wait and see!

Iris and Yechezkel would go to see Jack and found him again in the therapy room. Nancy asked whether the two little physical therapy assistants would be coming; Jack reacted well to them.

They made a call and Ari and Moishi were brought by Isaac and Sophie to hopefully help the clay process along. Sophie actually brought the boys to the therapy room; Isaac would return for them in about one hour. Sophie stood looking at Alex the therapist – staring and staring- but saying nothing. Not like her at all; working for a Rabbi, where people come with all sorts of issues-you were trained to do and be discreet and invisible. Not to stare, ask questions or make anyone uncomfortable. Certainly not in a hospital, in another city with someone so very elderly and fragile. The Rebbetzin noticed Sophie's reaction and tucked it away; with other impressions that she was storing! Sophie corrected herself so there was no need for the Rebbetzin to comment immediately anyway.

The Rebbe for himself had limited time and a big task. The discussion of what would happen after the summer and how Yaakov and Raizel would fare was a big concern. Bluma reaching out from the past, for her Yaakov seemed to be clarified. The question was about the baby blanket she was cradling. It seemed possible, no almost probable, that the baby and Yaakov were NOT one and the same! While time was flying; careful steps had to be planned to protect a fragile elderly person and his family.

The Rebbetzin had noticed a resemblance between Shana and Raizel and then dismissed it as trying

to make puzzle pieces fit. She tried to forget
Nancy's commenting on similarities, especially
their thick auburn hair. The Rebbe however
discouraged her from doubting her instincts. Both
had noticed other resemblances also. He had
commented again that all female names in this
group of women were flowers. Why Bluma reached
out to this Shana wasn't a coincidence; no such
thing as random or coincidence in Hashem's
designs.

There had to be some sort of diary or calendar or
record that Jack and his wife had kept; some
history for Lily and then Raizel. He would have
to find a non-threatening way to find out.

Time was getting short; his Gabbai had called a
few times about serious matters accumulating in
Cleveland. Besides Elul was fast upon them and
the Rebbe was needed by his kehillah for Selichos
and preparation for Rosh Hashana and Yomim
Noraiim.

Hashem's {Almighty's}

Elul {Name of Jewish month before High Holy Days}

Kehillah {congregation}

Selicho {special prayers recited week before Jewish New Year
and days before Day of Atonement}

Rosh Hashanah {Jewish New Year]

Yomim Noraiim {days of awe between Rosh Hashanah and Yom
Kippur- Day of Atonement}

This was the most serious time in the Jewish calendar and all needed their religious leader! The Levy family would also have to return to their Cleveland lives.

Jack/Yaakov would either be in this facility or a rehabilitation center; he was nowhere near well enough to return home and live independently. The question was Raizel- leave her as they'd found her, sitting days on end waiting for her Poppa to heal and hope R'Berel and his wife Rifka would be able to step in and fill gaps; or find another solution. The Rebbe knew he could advocate for his people much better from his home base; he was mightily hampered here in Skokie. However, he didn't want to jump to conclusions. If Jack was Yaakov and open to relocating, the Rebbe could see if Nurse Nancy was amenable to relocating and working privately. He would like to be able to continue to care for this family, so alone in the world and so beaten. A more realistic plan was to be sure there was good medical attention here in familiar surroundings. The money either way would work itself out; the Rebbe had wealthy Chasidim.

The therapist also looked very competent and was making strides with Yaakov if it was in fact Yaakov, son of Bluma. Either way, this was a Yiddish Kint and the Rebbe would take him under his wing. Raizel was a yesoma and as such, she needed the protection of this Rabbi's household.

Chasidim {devoted followers}

Yesoma {orphan}

In the interim, the Rebbe would see to leave adequate funds with R'Berel so he could act on the Rebbe's behalf to advocate for both Bakers, once all returned to Cleveland.

The pressure of time flying and many details to fulfill weighed heavily on the Cleveland contingent. It was decided that the next dinner Raizel would also attend and it would be the time to ask questions. The Rebbe and his wife would also privately bring Raizel into the picture so to speak.

Before that Mrs. Levy had requested some time. The Rebbetzin could only imagine how trying these days had been. Iris told her that Raizel had voiced legitimate questions and that she hadn't known how much to tell her.

The Rebbetzin suggested they wait until after this evening's dinner; Raizel would be in attendance and then perhaps after, answers and the way to present them would become clearer.

Raizel did in fact leave the hospital earlier than her regular pattern, to join in the dinner. Sophie served and then the boys were taken out by their parents. The Rebbetzin fussing with some compote, asked Raizel if they could look at the album again. The Rebbe sat quietly while Raizel asked her own questions. Only the truth, painful as it was would do.

The Rebbetzin though suggested that perhaps the Rebbe also look at the album and any other keepsake items Raizel felt comfortable in sharing.

Raizel *quickly re-visits her own thoughts and feelings as she goes upstairs to find keepsakes as requested. She decides she will also give him Poppa's journal; it seems the right time to do so. She trusts their motives and efforts to help!*

She's gone from sitting alone for months, watching her almost comatose Poppa, with Nancy spending some time to also meeting a kind understanding therapist. Alex was the most consistent therapist and in the early days after the stroke, he would come in and either exercise and massage Poppa's arms and legs or show the nurses how to do it. He would explain in plain English what Poppa's status was and what was a reasonable prognosis. Sounded grim and frightening to her; her world was shattering.

He noticed the room devoid of cards, flowers but more importantly people. Only the young girl, Raizel, who would sometimes be talking to her Poppa and sometimes reading. He offered a realistic prognosis and suggested ways she could enrich her own life, despite this crisis. With her experience with her Poppa, she could visit others and either spell them for a bit or just listen.

Suddenly visitors; first a Rabbi Berel and his wife and then a family from Cleveland. A visit first and then a stay for the summer, in the Baker home. They brought life to her sad and drab existence. They had a daughter about twelve or thirteen, mature but also on the quiet side.

Raizel couldn't have articulated why she was more of an observer than a participant in life but maybe it came of being raised by grandparents who were very quiet and filled with loss and pain. More than her parents' deaths; and that would have been more than enough.

The summer was certainly saved by the Levy family and it looked like Poppa was turning a corner. Recovery wouldn't be full but in time, he could learn to take care of his basic hygiene and he had financial benefits and they could and would live frugally. She would work and take care of him and it would work out because it had to.

She was grateful for small blessings; Nancy was kind and Alex thoughtful and she'd have to land on her feet when the Levy crew returned to Cleveland. Due to their care, a Grand Rabbi has come and a couple that has traveled with him. They take care of the home he is renting and are very outgoing and giving type of people. Sophie is a people nurturer and her husband makes all details of life, glide easily.

I was told if I needed something, to feel comfortable to ask them and I would. Iris though took care of all details so I didn't have to ask. I notice that Sophie keeps looking at Alex. One day in my Poppa's room and then one day in the therapy room, she was staring until Rebbetzin Sima touched her shoulder. I noticed her shaking her head as if to clear cobwebs from her mind.

Alex doesn't originally come from Skokie but I know, I've asked him- he's never been to Cleveland so it can't be that she knows him.

Things have moved very quickly these last few days. I didn't understand why all the attention. I mean the Levy family changed their entire summer plans *to come here; Shana told me this. Their renting the house really has been a gift, but why would people do something like this for a virtual stranger?*

Then this great Rabbi coming. R'Berel told me this Rabbi is world renowned, first in Europe and then in America. He's another one, R'Berel since Passover, constantly in touch and visiting; trying to lighten my load. This great Rebbe has throngs of people lining up to receive advice and a blessing from him, and women come from far and wide to bare their souls to his wife. She is the gentlest soul; huge loving eyes and a restful spirit. Around her, one feels loved and that all problems can and actually will evaporate. They are very humble and unassuming for world renowned folk!

They will leave soon, all of them, and it will be harder to return to the demands and the emptiness of my days. I will have to find work to help support our household and then care for Poppa. I am frightened.

My Poppa, he's changing though- and it's not just waking up from the coma. His eyes are more alive; they follow the people and the conversations. He is doing better with therapy and Nancy said, next step was the rehab section of the hospital.

Nancy also overheard me talking to Poppa and she said she'd remain in my life and be there for me. That I was a rare daughter/granddaughter and I would be o.k., Cleveland people or not. It seemed to her this Rabbi Berel would stay in touch.

Alex concurred so I felt encouraged and "wait and see" was a good mantra. I was good at waiting and

observing. Up until this summer and now I have new
questions daily.

All these thoughts upstairs while the Rebbe and
Rebbetzin waited for me. They must have thought
I'd fallen asleep or was avoiding sharing. I race
down the stairs and apologize- I was feeling very
overwhelmed. They nod in understanding.

They again look at the pictures and odds/ends I've
brought down. Most time was spent on the battered
"journal", wrapped in paper and tied with string.
This was Poppa's personal information; I was only
to handle if absolutely necessary or an emergency.
I decided this meeting qualified. I had thought
this great man would answer some of the questions
that I had posed to Iris. He asked for a little
time. The Rebbetzin senses my distress and tells
me that all will work out- to be patient for just
a bit longer. She sometimes calls me "shein
kint".

With that endearment, I feel protected and believe
it will all work out; the Rebbe will keep his word
no matter how many issues he juggles or how busy
he is. For me, it has to be face to face so I can
absorb information from him and then express what
is troubling me. The Levy's have another two weeks
and they'll pack up and leave.

Shein kint {dear child}

Their place in my life has grown and I hope we will remain in touch. I sense that Iris too has questions; she has more opportunity for satisfaction though, as she lives in Cleveland.

I hope at the end I will have clarity so that this summer wouldn't be like a dream from which I'd have to wake up. Only the truth will enable me to finally stop floating and begin living and coping.

Next day, next step in the Rebbe's carefully crafted approach. The Rebbetzin along with Sophie went to meet with Nancy. They told the nurse that they had some more information that was sensitive and might affect Jack Baker. All know Jack is a fragile person; the Rebbe and his wife know how very fragile the process is. They want to find out the soonest day and most auspicious time, to have another conversation with Jack. It will be handled gently, only up to the point that Jack can handle it well.

Checking his vitals Nancy said, "Mid- morning was fine up to mid -afternoon." Nancy trusted this Rabbi, having witnessed his intuitive approach; she would be in attendance however to make sure Jack was strong enough for anything out of the ordinary. All knew Jack tired very easily and emotional issues exhausted him, even more so.

Isaac brought the Rebbe and Iris brought Shana; Raizel was in her position by her Poppa's side. Nancy checked Jack's vitals and gave the green light.

The Rebbe said he would again speak first in Yiddish and then he would continue in English. He asked that all listen carefully and then the Rebbetzin and he would meet individually with Shana, Raizel and Mrs. Levy, at different times.

All would receive the answers to questions that they deserved. He thanked them for their patience and trust.

The Rebbe began by reminding Yaakov how much his mother must have loved him and how very hard it would have been for her to be unable to protect her son. Some words in the journal indicate she'd

91

been beaten trying to keep her little boy away from the soldiers or wannabe soldiers; she never would recover from these wounds, both physical and emotional.

Rebbe continues in his melodious voice; "What could she say – what **one thing** that maybe he would remember and carry with him always. He was so very little and he had just started learning the Aleph Bais (Hebrew alphabet); so, what could she tell him?" She thought quickly and told him, **"Yaakov, Gedenk di bist a yid- Gedenk Modeh Ani** and **Gedenk Shmah Yisrael.**"

Yaakov was crying and nodding ever so slightly, as if to say yes, yes.

The Rebbe continued that Yaakov must wonder how does a Rebbe today even know this and why is this all happening - now?

"A young girl, Shana Levy in Cleveland began seeing an image of an old grandmotherly type, with babushka, in a large room crying and begging.

She would try to tell Shana that something had happened to her son, spelling out her name by introduction and then her son's name and trying to make Shana understand a rifle was involved.

Aleph Bais {Jewish alphabet}

Her tears were not just for this child; she was constantly rocking a baby blanket, in a pastel color with a little bit of embroidery in one corner. This happened over quite a number of visits via mirror.

Young Shana tried to ignore the upsetting images but this woman, Bluma wouldn't let up. She was persistent and Shana and her parents finally came to me, to try to figure out what this Bluma was trying to convey, and why. As if to break the tension, the Rebbe says, "It's been an unbelievable journey; we have met a caring R'Berel, your wonderful Raizel and Nurse Nancy and the therapist Alex."

The Rebbe then returns to the subject at hand. "You, Yaakov, know this to be true because the first time this young Shana stood by your bed, the mirror in her purse rattled and your mother's identical words came out of Shana's mouth; in your mother's voice and accent!

You were never forgotten and your mother doesn't want you to forget, she has repeated **"Gedenk Die Bist a Yid"**.

I can't say for certain why Bluma chose this young girl; it is possible her soul has tried before and was ignored OR that her Neshama was granted the ability at this one time to reach out. It is also possible she sensed you were deathly ill and she reached out at the same time. We know if you are her son, she has a great granddaughter Raizel, who needs to learn about her heritage and her great grandmother's instructions and wishes."

The Rebbetzin took advantage of the pause in the Rebbe's words to translate to those that didn't understand English. The mirror wasn't mentioned in the translation.

Nurse Nancy stood shocked at this recitation. Her training though stood her in good stead, and she checked Jack's pulse and asked for a brief break. At least she understood- or thought she did- what had happened the first time Shana had visited; it hadn't been her fault at all! It was a soul trying to find peace and give peace.

Raizel was holding the Rebbetzin's hand, holding on to tangible comfort while processing a story that seemed surreal.

Iris though wasn't comforted. Something was missing.

The Rebbe continued speaking in Yiddish. "Yaakov, I have to return to my Cleveland shul and many obligations. It will soon be Rosh Hashana. You will improve slowly – I give you a brocha for a Refuah Shlaima. I don't however think it's good for Raizel to return every night to the empty house. The Levy's have to return home as well. We would like to invite Raizel to stay in Cleveland, until after the Yomim Tovim.

She will be well looked after

Refuah Shlaima {complete recovery} Yomim

Tovim {holidays}

We will be in touch with Nurse Nancy and Alex and perhaps try to arrange for private care so you can continue your treatment and hopefully recover more quickly.

R'Berel will be in touch with you and with me; **I won't abandon you. My word, bli neder- no matter what**!" The Rebbe had in mind to try to do further research, overseas, to be sure his advice would be as accurate as feasible and fulfill a tormented soul's wishes!

Yaakov shook his head as if to say "yes" and the Rebbe translated the last basic details to Raizel, adding "if you are willing to come for this type of visit."

Raizel looked at her Poppa, who blinked and slowly nodded to her and she with her own tears answered that she would come to Cleveland in a few weeks. She wanted to spend more time with her Poppa and she had to close the house up.

Iris would discuss this with Yechezkel but she was fairly certain he would agree that they invite Raizel to join them. There was one small room they could fix up for her and perhaps she could observe and absorb some important tenets of Judaism, especially during the upcoming serious time of New Year holidays.

Bli neder {one's word, but not a vow}

The raw emotions and repercussions of actions taken are heavy loads to carry. The Rebbe and Rebbetzin aren't as young as they once were or would like to be. Spiritual and emotional energy siphon off from physical stamina; this type of process leaves neither in abundance. One entire day off after returning, was scheduled for them to switch gears. They both took more time with their tefilos and recitation of Tehilim; begging for added insights to direct their actions for the good of all. The Gabbai returned phone calls and set up easier scheduling for the first week until the Rebbe was back to the rhythm of Cleveland schedule.

Yaakov, Raizel, Iris and Shana were not forgotten by far.

Many calls were placed to Reb Berel who was happy to facilitate communication with Yaakov Bekker and the Rebbe. Arrangements were being made for Raizel to come spend the next few months in Cleveland. She would stay with the Levy's but she would spend much time around the Rebbetzin and Sophie; certainly, for Yomim Noraiim. Sophie was freshening up the little corner room, Isaac would paint it in Raizel's favorite color which was lavender.

She'd be taken shopping so that she had appropriate clothing for holidays and some shul attendance, if only to hear the blowing of the Shofar, and all had to be done with sensitivity, leaving her feeling nurtured, dignified and not beholden.

Shofar {ram's horn}

Iris and the entire family had taken to her so it wasn't difficult at all to include her in their family and introduce her to their Cleveland life. She was interested now in reasons for all they did. As her Poppa's first post stroke words were Modeh Ani, she undertook to say these. What would naturally follow would be Netilas Yodayim and she learned this as well. The brocha that followed the hand washing hopefully would come later. The theme she observed was recognition of Hashem/ our Higher Power and being grateful **to Him** and **for Him** in our lives at the first step and every step. She knew if she continued on this path, that she had so very much to learn. All told her to learn step by step, little by little and NOT look at what she didn't know or needed to learn. It would be overwhelming and discouraging any other way, and this, no one wanted.

Iris was biding her time; she'd been told that the Rebbe and Rebbetzin would meet with her after the Succos Yom Tov ended and the massive Succah

Modeh Ani {morning prayer- I thank Almighty}

Netilas Yadayim {ritual hand washing, immediate upon awakening}

brocha {blessing}

Succah {temporary hut built for the holiday)

would be dismantled. She was patient because she was afraid of upheaval that some of the information would bring. There was no turning back though.

The weather had become chilly. Isaac was out in the windy weather, building the Rebbe's huge succah to accommodate the many Chassidim that would make the brocha on the lulav / esrog, in the succah. Sophie ran upstairs and tried to find one of his scarves; appropriate for this weather and not the very heavy wool types that he only wore in winter's frigid and sub- zero conditions.

As she was tossing the contents of the catch all drawer around, she found a few old pictures, black and white, a bit creased and edges cracked. She'd have to organize this drawer was her first thought. Reminiscing for a moment she saw that one was a young Isaac and this stopped her in her tracks. Proof to her that what she saw as a resemblance between Alex in Skokie and her Isaac now, was supported by the photo. One could have mistaken one for the other, except for the dated clothing Isaac was wearing.

She ran down, picture in her apron pocket and handed Isaac the scarf.

Brocha {blessing}

Lulav/esrog {palm branch and citron}

He saw she was upset but she waved him away saying she'd bring him a thermos of tea very soon. In the meantime, she went to find the Rebbetzin and show her the picture.

The Rebbetzin hadn't needed proof; she had seen the resemblance; the Rebbe had as well. They hadn't commented on it. They both remembered their younger Isaac and they also knew what both Sophie and Isaac couldn't; there was a painful back story for how Isaac became their "son".

Day to day living brought questions and upset. For the generations of survivors, much more so. Always the quandary, whether to open up wounds that had healed over; albeit with scarring or advise people to move on/ move forward, without opening upsets.

First priority though, were Yaakov and Raizel and how their true history affected others. Raizel was doing well; worried about her Poppa but speaking to him and writing him while also conversing with Nancy. Nancy was a very good nurse and now that Jack was her sole patient; she devoted herself fully to his total care. Home care was decided upon; his own surroundings would help him emotionally which would hasten other recoveries. A woman her age and stage; this was a good job for her as she got older and she wanted to do right by the opportunity. She'd learned much about devotion, meeting R'Berel first and then Iris Levy and then the Grand Rabbi and His Wife! She, Alex and Jack were a team, offering him great incentive to improve daily.

Jack's speech was slow and becoming somewhat clearer; remembering nouns and simple vocabulary, week by week. He was mastering the use of the spoon and fork and able to feed himself if the food was cut in small bites. Neat eating would come in time! Every advance was savored, coming after much repetitive therapy designed for each task!   Exercise daily and he was now using a walker to slowly make his way across the living room and dining room areas. Each day he was able to take more steps. Rugs had been picked up and flooring had been washed but not waxed, to avoid slips. He tired easily, used the wheel chair but each day spent a bit more "walking". Truly a step by step emotional and physical recovery and journey!

The aim was that Jack be able to dress himself, shave and re-learn how to read and then write as well as eat on his own. Hygiene, in small steps; teeth brushing, hand / face washing and then onto showering with some helpful tools. This was work that might take years.

No mention of Shana or Bluma; too risky. If he would be able to ask, then maybe and then only with the Rebbe's guidance. Nancy though would find Jack staring far into space, with tears coursing down his cheeks. She would pat his shoulder saying "I know Jack- I heard".

Any and all progress is relayed to both R'Berel and Raizel. She in turn speaks to Iris and/or the Rebbetzin and Sophie daily.

The long- awaited appointment for Iris and Yechezkel has finally arrived. Shana is aware that her parents are going to speak with the Rebbe. She's watching Ari and Moishi and for once bedtime is easy. If they are asleep, she can invite a friend over but she has to leave the phone clear.

Shana is too edgy to socialize anyway; she will finish her homework and then draw or write. This meeting brings back all the times she saw this Bluma in the mirror and it reminds her of the uncertainty and changes in their lives. She can readily admit how frightening Bluma became, with each appearance, trying to give her information.

Raizel actually accompanied her parents and that too was fine with Shana. There were times they really got along and there were others where there seemed to be a wedge between them; unspoken but there.

The Gabbai escorts the trio straight into the kitchen and there is hot cocoa for Raizel, coffee, tea and some sugar cookies on the tray.

The Rebbe begins by thanking them for their patience, waiting to be helped to make sense of all. He asks Raizel how she is doing and will she remain in Cleveland longer than the agreed upon holidays? Raizel says "She'd like to go back to Skokie for a while, spend time with her Poppa and then see if she can return." The Rebbetzin pats her shoulder and says, "It's very understandable that she misses her Poppa."

The Rebbe having begun a relaxed dialogue starts speaking about some Neshamos /(souls) that don't have the menucha that we imagine there is in shomayim. This Bluma had two children seemingly and both were lost to her; one by circumstance of the Cantonist evil decrees and one due to ill health and her being an older widow. The pain of losing her Yaakov, when she tried desperately to protect him, was overwhelming to her. No son, and her husband rarely able to come home. When she found herself again expecting a baby, she was happy- new life and new hope. However, she was advised that her husband had been killed as a soldier fighting and she was left alone with an infant girl.

This all extrapolated from registry records overseas- taking much time, which accounts for the delay in this meeting.

Menucha {peaceful rest}

Shomayim {heaven}

What Shana saw, Bluma in the mirror, holding a
pastel colored blanket with stitching in one
corner was alluding to this infant. Shana
couldn't decipher the lettering, but in one brief
mirror visit, it was there, tiny and almost
unnoticed: "ayin", "raish", "yud" and "samach" —
Iris {pronounced Eris in Hebrew}-a Hebrew name of
a flower." Yechezkel nods but remains quiet-
subtly and carefully observing his wife's
reactions.

The Rebbetzin continued that the journal described
her painful decision and choosing a set of
neighbors, younger than she, who couldn't have
children and that could and would provide for a
baby. She gave the baby to them, asking that they
care for this child as their own, but to please
keep her name, and honor their religion. The name
they kept; however, when this family was able to
leave Europe; their commitment to Yiddishkeit
slipped away. They came to America and lovingly
raised this little Iris though.

At some point the journal was buried, but mention
of Bluma's daily fervent tefilos and tears were
noted. She would take care of her children in
this- the only way available to her!

{Letters corresponding phonetically eris}

Tefilos {prayers}

Iris breaks in asking "Is that Iris me?" The Rebbetzin answers: "As far as we can surmise, the answer is yes. On the few legible pages of the Bekker journal, there are those very same letters written, no explanation, in what seems to be shaky handwriting. You were adopted and given very little information. We have noticed a resemblance between Raizele and your Shana for one thing. Also, Bubba Bluma appeared in the mirror of a grandchild to implore her to pay attention and take notice and help!

"As we are on this subject and together, we received a call yesterday. R'Berel had been summoned to Yaakov's house. Jack had been sitting up, working on trying to brush his teeth and was visited via mirror by Bluma. It would seem she was standing, pointing her finger and saying "Yaakov, **Shmah Yisroel**! She was holding a pastel colored baby blanket. She then faded out. In this visit, Nancy was also able to see an image, not Jack's reflection and also remembering these same words that she'd heard previously. Jack then kept trying to repeat those two words.

"He kept repeating her instruction and crying Mamme Mamme. He / they saw and heard what Shana had seen."

Raizel raised her hand and asks, "Does this mean that Iris is my Poppa's sister, making her like my aunt and the Levy children my cousins?" The Rebbetzin answers "Yes, you are all mishpucha /blood. Iris will work with Nancy to find the right time and way(s) to tell Yaakov- there was a sister, Iris Levy is the sister. She is the baby that Bluma was trying to call attention to, by using a baby blanket; the sister he never knew.

104

Now he's trying to heal and he's also dealing with images and reminders of his dear mother! In time he can handle this all!

"In the right time, we will also speak with Shana. Iris and Yechezkel should assure her of this. She will have questions that we will do our best to answer. It is best that we do so after you have processed the facts, we believe are true, have become comfortable with them as they change your own histories."

The Rebbe continues, "It would be then good to suggest that Yaakov relocate and if he's amenable, we will work out the many details. If and when he is ready, we can begin to make arrangements for Yaakov, Nancy and maybe even Alex to make the move to Cleveland." Raizel brightens with the mention of Alex.

All are silent; reliving the efforts over generations of a Mother who didn't rest until she brought her family "home". The Levy's both realize how painstakingly difficult the Rebbe's work is, and they are only one tiny segment of what this holy man juggles.

Iris had to get used to the idea of closure now. Her entire life she wondered why she was given up for adoption. It had been like a hole in her being, despite good adoptive parents and a wonderful husband. Now she knew her Mother had no choice and she had davened and cared throughout time. Closure and new openings; rich family ties; much to handle simultaneously.

She understood now. Her mother had wanted the best for her and had done her best under challenging conditions. Her choices were not easy; she'd made the best one she could. She couldn't know that America sometimes made Yidden abandon their religion or dilute it. Iris wouldn't judge; her adoptive parents had done their best for her as well. Thankfully, Iris had become a Baalas Teshuva, met Yechezkel in that journey and was raising her family devoutly observant.

More thankfully though, the Rebbe and Rebbetzin would speak to Shana. Shana thankfully was happy with that, patient with their process and asked no questions despite seeing new closeness between her mother and Raizel. She also didn't miss a new lightness in her mother. The Rebbetzin said they would meet with Shana, all together, and tell her. They would have the right words, timing and certainly perfect touch as they would address the why she was chosen as Bluma's messenger. Shana would always carry the weight of being the receiver of the mirror message. It changed her from a young carefree adolescent girl into someone more serious.

Balaas Teshuva {returnee to observance}

She'd experienced something that very few if any, ever did.

In a small community, especially observant, many would question the sudden appearance of family. The Rebbe suggested that Iris say that she had been searching for any information about her birth parents and ads placed, led her to finding living relatives.

The truth, but not in its entirety; and the rest of the how and where, were family private matters. All involved were happy to agree to this.

The Gabbai was entrusted to update R'Berel who finally with his wife understood, the entire dynamic of the Levy family coming to Skokie and followed by the Grand Rebbe, et al, resulting with a brother, sister and their children identified as family.

Arrangements to find space and an appropriate set up for Yaakov and Nancy first - with space for Raizel was left to the Gabbai and Isaac. Nancy would discuss Alex's plans for Cleveland; being a larger city; there were better study and work opportunities here that could further his career if he so chose. If not, ads would be placed to interview therapists that Jack could work well with. Nancy was fairly sure he had incentives to accept the opportunity though.

Sophie and the picture would have to wait. The Rebbetzin asked the Gabbi to clear any appointments for a specific Tuesday calendar if feasible; she had a personal matter that needed the Rebbe's attention. All she needed to say was that it related to time in Europe when his older brother was Rebbe and the Gabbai said he'd be available whenever, no matter what, more than

107

always. He had been with the prior Rebbe as well and knew some of the sad history. Constant rush of people, in and then out, showing the emotions of anxiety, worry, pain and possible relief, were a Gabbai's world, especially in the tense pre-World War II European cities. He remembered twin sisters and then twin sons, a revolving door of Shailos. The resolution then had resulted in serious repercussions for many!

Keeping things from her revered husband wasn't the Rebbetzin's way but she needed to protect his gezunt. She told Sophie that in the right time, the matter would be discussed. Once she showed him the picture, it would open up painful wounds. Once the Succos holiday ended, the Rebbe returned to the regular schedule was the most optimum time to open up this "story".

The appointed day finally arrived and the Rebbetzin did what for her was tried and true; a delicious soup and some crackers. She reminded the Rebbe that Sophie had had some type of recognition of Alex, the therapist in Skokie facility. The Rebbetzin slowly takes out the picture and shows the Rebbe.

The Rebbe looks at it, tears streaming out of his eyes and says "I didn't need to see this. I knew in my heart. A mirror and a desperate mother both lead to another thread of history, our own pain, not only Bluma's and Yaakov's."

Shailos {important questions - Jewish rule or direction}

Gezunt {health}

A Rebbe carries many stories and is able to compartmentalize, and give each family/person and each situation, undivided attention to focus, pray and advise. Now though, one of the stories involves his past and present loved ones.

The Rebbetzin sits quietly and waits while the Rebbe paces and composes himself. Some things can be buried, some can't be pushed ahead of the perfect time and some can't and won't be denied. She reminisces as she is sure her husband is; returning to his and their young years, as the younger brother of a great Rebbe, from a dynasty of world renowned Rebbes. A different continent, style of observing Judaism, steeped in centuries of this type of devotion, and changing political climate which again, became ominous for the Jews.

A time so totally different than Judaism in America. In Europe, a Rebbe was the focal point of Jewish life. Most questions - whether halachic or emotional issues- were matters to consult with the Rebbe. In America, not as much, but devotees of a Rebbe, relied much on their religious leader.

The spirit of the holiness of their Rebbe elevated their decisions; they followed their leader's customs **and if** they asked, they followed his advice. Times of trouble, they flocked to him. Times of joy, He would be included. He carried their troubles on his shoulders, praying to Hashem /Almighty for divine guidance.

Halachic {Torah tenets}

So many stories that were never shared; all had to be held in utmost confidence.

One tragedy though affected the Rebbe's older brother, at that time, the Rebbe of the city, and by default this current Rebbe's own life. They had closed the book on this for decades. Rebuilding vibrant Jewish communities with Yeshivas and shuls in a new country, new culture and new language was every Rabbi's "avoda". One Chassidus especially, like the one to which R'Berel belonged, devoted their time to actively seeking out Yiddish kinder/children, any background, and try to bring them back to any level of observance. They were known for their "outreach".

All clergy, every background and level, were very involved in the needs of each family within the community, ensuring that the lifestyles in Golus wouldn't infect the impressionable children and lead them astray.

America that had been a haven for so many, that ran from the ashes of Europe wasn't to be mistaken as spiritually safe. Changes in the upbringing of youth (too permissive) and wild immodest behavior were plaguing parents of all strata, each year more and more!

Yeshivas {Jewish study halls}

Avoda {mission}

Golus {diaspora}

The Rebbe is thinking; to have to re-visit the most difficult "shaila"/question, an emotional dilemma brought to my older brother who was a very sensitive and understanding Rebbe is like a nightmare for my Rebbetzin and me. I never wanted to be a leader. I wanted to study, perhaps author holy Talmudic commentaries and try to help people quietly. However, often life doesn't offer choices. Now the nightmare challenge of his Rabbinate is begging me for immediate attention.

The Rebbe returns to the scenario; in the community in Rumania/Hungary there were twin sisters that had married and remained living in the same town. The husbands were compatible; working and studying. Avrum Zilber and his wife Hinda were blessed with children and in fact, were awaiting a Simcha in a few months. Yehuda nick-named Yidel Reich and his wife Leba, Hinda's twin, were married for about ten years but not yet blessed.

Leba was desperate to have children. She asked her sister Hinda to allow her to adopt this newborn and she promised she and Yidel would raise this child with love, with material ease and with Yiddishkeit in the way Hinda and Avrum were raising their children. Hinda would be close by and be able to watch her child, that would become her niece or nephew- thrive.

Hinda loved her sister and would do anything for her sister, or so she thought. To give away her very own child, not that!

Simcha {blessed-happy occasion}

She spoke to her husband Avrum and he wasn't in favor of this at all. In fact, he felt it was a huge chutzpa (nerve) for Leba to even have uttered a request such as this. They with their growing family however should at least be compassionate for the childless state of Leba/Yidel and give it a little thought.

Leba though, once she said it the first time more easily repeated it at any and every opportunity, she and Hinda were together. It was becoming the only conversation until Avrum told Hinda and Leba that they could only get together, if this wasn't mentioned at all!

Yehuda began to like the idea; he also wanted a family and it looked like this could be the answer to their tefilos. He would badger Avrum until the once very close relationship between the two families became strained.

Hinda was very busy with her other children and was more house bound. Leba stopped by, ostensibly with some soup and kugel, but in fact to make a suggestion. Leba told Hinda she knew she was asking a lot, but she was desperate. Perhaps they should go to the Rebbe and put this on the table. If the Rebbe said no, "No it would be." If the Rebbe thought it might be a good idea, perhaps Hinda and Avrum would re-consider and find a way to make this loving sacrifice.

An appointment with the very sought after Rebbe was made and someone to watch over Hinda's other kinderlich was found.

Tefilos {prayers}

A wagon, to accommodate both couples, was engaged and the two couples set out to meet with the Godol.

Godol {great Jewish Rabbi or personality}

The Gabbai, Shalom, was instructed to lighten the day's appointments for only the urgent issues. The Rebbetzin didn't leave the Rebbe's side as he was reminiscing. All was now precipitated by the photo that Sophie had located which confirmed her observation; Alex was somehow related to her Isaac.

A photo, a person, a dream; whatever method Hashem employed to bring issues to the forefront of a memory or thought; the Rebbe knew all was from Hashem and he would have to deal with this now.

His brother had shared the issue involving the Zilber and Reich families, when handing over the responsibility-the mantle of being the Rebbe. Otherwise the secret would have remained sealed.

His brother, the Rebbe in Rumania was going to meet with the twin sisters and their husbands. The Rebbetzin would be in the room; that was the custom. If a Rebbe was meeting with women, his wife, the Rebbetzin would be there so the meeting would continue; comfortably if wives were involved and appropriately for all. The Rebbetzin could also be a source of support and offer her own insight, if called upon.

The very unusual question was set forth   The Rebbe then could see that Hinda and Avrum only came to ask out of consideration for their siblings. They were uncomfortable with the shaila even being uttered. Leba and Yidel offered compelling arguments for the adoption. They had the means to do right by a child; they so desperately wanted; a baby and Hinda and Avrum could watch the progress of their child.   It was the only way. To adopt a child with uncertain background and yichus; this they couldn't do.

The Rebbe spoke to each couple separately and understood, to deny someone, especially a sibling/twin such a request was very difficult. Avrum and Hinda were pious, devout and kind people and didn't know if this was a sacrifice they should stretch to do, or if they were permitted to say no, in good conscience. They sensed that their familial relationship might be broken if they were unable to make this supreme sacrifice; Leba wouldn't be able to forgive her sister for denying her, her heart's desire.

Leba and Yidel on the other hand felt that there could be no other answer than yes. If they couldn't receive this child, this chance for a family, there would be a permanent break in the shalom of the family. They wouldn't want that to happen, but it would be a sad result. Hinda and Avrum could make them parents or break the relationship!

The Rebbe said he would think about this and send a message when there was an answer.

In the interim, Hinda gave birth, to twin boys. Leba elated felt this was a sign. One for Leba and one for Hinda, and Yidel voiced this same reasoning, when visiting the Rebbe.

Yichus {lineage}

Shalom {peace}

The bris of each was delayed until they were deemed healthy and large enough. One boy was named Naftali and the other Yitzchak. Hinda put the dilemma on the back burner; there were not enough hours in the day to tend to the crying infants and the needs of the other little ones.

Leba had time on her hands and offered to come and help; it would have been a blessing but Hinda demurred. No way did she want Leba to become attached to any of the infants and use the time to keep pressuring her.

The Rebbe for himself had no night and no day. He began cancelling meetings with people who would travel for hours and days to meet with him. His tisch was less long in duration and this Rebbe was totally preoccupied. The question was difficult enough when it involved only one child. Now there were twins and for Yidel and Leba, that seemed proof of the rightness of their wish. Hashem's perfect solution, no?

To give away a child though; so very difficult. How could anyone be expected to do this?

The Rebbe fasted, he cried and he davened and then finally sent a message that he would meet with the couples and the set of twins. Leba and Yidel were sure they would prevail.

Bris {circumcision usually takes place baby's 8th day}

Tisch {table where devotees are received}

Davened {prayed}

Hinda and Avrum decided the test for them so far would be if they could fulfill, something seemingly unthinkable, that a Rebbe would direct.

The Rebbe wouldn't give a psak. He would outline options. Life as it was would change. The seeds of an Amalek were evident in the politics of the time. Yidden were always targeted; the first to suffer. One could only do one's honest best and adhere to the tenets of the Torah, no matter what! There were no guarantees except the present/ today /now and doing one's best in each moment and situation. This was his preamble.

The Rebbe and Rebbetzin met with the two families and spoke: "To give up a child is a huge decision. It would show great **mesiras nefesh** for family; an over the top act of chesed. Should Hinda and Avrum be able to give one of the boys, it would be with the solemn pact that this child would always be raised totally observant. If, however, they were not able to make this huge sacrifice, they would be doing nothing wrong. This wasn't a chiyuv. Threatening them with breaking Shalom wasn't correct, fair or a factor in this weighty decision.

Psak {decision or ruling}

Amalek {historical name of Jewish nemesis}

Mesiras nefesh {ultimate sacrifice or devotion}

Chesed {kindness}

Chiyuv {obligatory legal requirement}

If they would allow Yidel and his wife to adopt the child, then Avrum and his wife would have to decide if it was better to maintain close logistical connection; or, if distance would be best for the adopted parents / child.

The Zilber family left, weighing the painful options. Most likely without the ability to adopt this infant, Leba and Yidel would have no children. On the other hand, to separate twin brothers no less and other siblings would be like cutting off a finger and cutting out a piece of the parents' hearts.

They both thought and weighed the matter and by the end of the week, they visited the Rebbe, asked for brochos and said they would give one, to be raised as a Reich, with the firm reiterated promise that he be raised as he would be if with his family of birth. The Rebbe absorbed their decision and advised them, that it be Naftuli, (Chassidic pronunciation) that they give. No reason given or understood.

Needless to say, each Reich was ecstatic, full of gratitude and reaffirming the promise that little Naftuli would be raised ehrlich.

Months passed; the climate in Europe for Yidden (Jews) wasn't promising. New rules each day; it seemed a noose was tightening. Mr. Reich decided to apply for visas to leave Rumania.

The process was costly and lengthy but he secured three visas. Their departure was emotional and the condition of adoption was again mentioned.

Brochos {blessings}

Ehrlich {devoutly}

"Gedenk, ehrtzie ayme ehrlich". Once papers were secured, one had to leave quickly and Hinda and Avrum had little time to internalize the reality that they would not be able to keep an eye on Naftali; they couldn't even contemplate not ever seeing him again. How would they find the financial means to secure a visa and money for a round trip when in these financially insecure times, they had no ability to even save any money at all?

No one could foresee that after the horrible years of the Nazi chokehold, the only two Zilber survivors of the Holocaust would be Yitzchak Zilber and Naftali Reich.

Yidel and Leba Reich came to the goldini medina and didn't want to be known as the "greener". They learned the language swiftly, worked hard to lose the European accent and set themselves up in a business, using most of the funds they had accrued in Europe. The U.S. media didn't cover the atrocities in Europe much, if at all and Yidel and Leba were unaware of the absolute reign of terror and carnage.

They lived well as Jules and Libby Richards and little Naftoli became known as Nate.   They didn't realize that by changing their names, anyone trying to find them, would find no trail.

Gedenk, ehrtzie ayme ehrlich" (remember to raise him observant}

Goldini medina {expression – land of gold- America}

Greener {immigrants}

In the sea of continuous changes, was Nate's Hebrew education which was sporadic afternoon Talmud Torah and this only until his Bar Mitzva.

Their fortunes would change though.

What happened to Yitzchak? He had been about three and again Hinda and Avrum were faced with difficult decisions. People were desperately trying to hide their children. The Church, no, that could only be the last option for them; the risk being the Church would baptize children in their care! They couldn't and wouldn't want to take a chance on the "chinuch" of their children. It would be impossible to reclaim, so no, only as the last resort. They'd lost touch with Leba and Yidel so a request for help with visas was not an option. Perhaps they would sell the last of their silver objects and with that money, pay someone to take their Yitzchak in and keep him safe. They would return for him. They could hide more easily without a little one who couldn't keep up. They had spoken to a kind trusted seamstress, and she and her husband promised to protect the little one.

Good plan- but they didn't return; not either of them nor their other children.

They had left a letter with the Rebbe outlining where Yitzchak was hidden. If for some reason they wouldn't be able to return, would the Rebbe take him under his wing and raise him as if he was their own? Perhaps the Rebbe would have ways to find the Reich family in America, believing that their other child was being raised in the agreed upon manner.

Chinuch {religious teaching - training}

If not would the Rebbe undertake the total care of their baby? The Rebbe, couldn't turn his back on this family and this child.

At this point as the Cleveland Rebbe was talking out loud and remembering this family's tzaara, the Rebbetzin interrupted him. It was somewhat after this incident that that Rebbe told his younger brother that he would not be able to continue as a religious leader. This story had cost him; he wasn't sure he had handled this correctly. Avrum and Hinda were fading in front of his eyes. He became weak, a shell of himself, and lost any confidence in his ability to guide anyone, even with simple questions. During excruciatingly brutal days and edicts, a younger brother, a new Rebbe, stepped in to minister to the myriad that were suffering. It was under this circumstance that this current Rebbe, painfully and reluctantly took the reins with Rebbetzin Sima as his wife. Brothers knew the only plus in this story was that one child was taken out of the gehinom Hitler was creating.

The older Rebbe brother sadly passed away carrying this burden and feeling ineffective as a leader! Passed away before round ups, train transports and incineration.

Tzaara {tragic circumstance}

Gehinom {purgatory}

The war years, men dragged off to work camps unable to communicate except for censored post cards. Women and children hungry and relocated first to crowded ghetto living and then to the "vagonen" for transport, worse than cattle, to Auschwitz and other camps of that ilk. This saintly couple and their children were separated and herded to various lines and selections, unable to find out who was given another day. What they did know though, when they accepted the mantle, was that if they survived and the Zilbers didn't, they would undertake full responsibility for finding Yitzchak and advocating for baby Yitzchak. They would try to find his relatives in America. If they couldn't, he would become their child. Many would wonder why no letter ever was received from the Reich family, once they left Rumania. That question would never be satisfied.

Perhaps there could be a way that the Rebbetzin and Rebbe could visit with Alex's parents. The Rebbetzin then chuckled, she was always getting ahead of herself.

Hard to fathom, even while living through the worst nightmare of all time, but most didn't return. This Rebbe and his Rebbetzin did, health adversely affected but spirit strong, ready to help their fellow Yidden (Jews) to rebuild.

The Zilbers and their other children didn't survive and it was left to the new Rebbe to claim young Yitzchak.

Vagonen {trains}

Europe was unwelcoming after the War- another emotional blow- and plans were made to leave, either to Eretz Yisroel/Israel or America, depending on acquiring documentation. After years, they had the necessary papers, and made their way to New York, first stop. They had not ceased inquiring about Leba and Yidel Reich in New York, and a few other major Jewish cities, to no avail. They honored their promise and Yitzchak had become their own child. Sophie had a similar history, from a different country and Yitzchak and Sophie would connect much later and be married. Both considered this Rabbi and his wife, their family; it was mutual!

The Rebbetzin was thinking as the Rebbe was. If we see the strong resemblance between Alex in Skokie and the Yitzchak we raised and who is here with us now, why didn't Alex? Why not Isaac? Sophie did though. Perhaps Isaac was never in the same space as Alex. I guess this solves one oddity; my Rebbe never travels with anyone but R'Shalom the Gabbai and here he was asked to hold the fort in Cleveland and we traveled with Isaac and Sophie. Otherwise Sophie wouldn't have been in a position to notice and I might have been distracted and not paid attention.

"Rebbe, another thought; why can't we put an ad in the nationally distributed paper also, like the Levy's were counseled to do. It could say we are looking for a Naftali Reich, parents Leba and Yehuda / Yidel and give our number."

The Rebbe answered, "This was already done with no results. The ad was run four times in various papers.

For the inquiry into a Yaakov Bekker, the mirror messenger was insistent and the search wasn't dropped. In this case, perhaps Sophie and Isaac should just carry on with no resolution; this may be the end of the road. We won't encourage Alex to relocate and perhaps we can contain this."

The Rebbetzin knew that this wouldn't happen; Raizel liked Alex. He had been very kind to her all those weeks, as she sat with her Poppa- before R'Berel, the Levy's and our visit.

The Rebbetzin then thought that perhaps asking Nurse Nancy who worked very closely with Alex, might yield some bits of helpful detail. Perhaps he will talk about his parents and family or has and then we might become better informed. The Rebbe approved of this suggestion for which the Rebbetzin was happy. She didn't want to give up - - because Sophie wouldn't or couldn't let it go! If Alex was a blood relative to their Yitzchak; they owed him this truth and shouldn't back away. They had to see this through to the end! She didn't have to share that this may be even more urgent than the Rebbe even realizes; enough time later on if clarity doesn't come quickly on its own.

If that wasn't a successful avenue, perhaps there could be a way that the Rebbetzin and Rebbe could visit with Alex's parents. The Rebbetzin then chuckled, she was always getting ahead of herself.

Jack was excited about relocating. He was becoming depressed in his home, with no Raizel to brighten his existence and to live for.

The few touches clearly evident from the Levy stay were nice, but now there was no life in this house. Little if anything to look forward to. Jack knew It was best for her to go forward; and the Levy's and the Rabbi had proven their devotion. He had to get used to the idea that Mrs. Levy, Iris, was actually his sister; albeit much younger. R'Berel and Nancy had revealed this to him, over a few conversations. At least his sister was spared the heart break of the Cantonist cruelty; she'd been nurtured by a family.

They had lifetimes to catch up on. He liked her boys and would come to know Shana despite their inauspicious first meeting - her blurting out words in his mother's voice and language.

Nancy was wonderful. He felt without her he wouldn't be progressing as steadily as he was. His speech was still slurring. It took him much time to express the simplest thoughts. He had to be careful with every step he took; but it was far better than the months he had lost due to his stroke.

Alex, he was good at his profession. He knew how far to encourage him and when to give him some down time. He would travel with them, visit Cleveland a bit and then who knew.

R'Berel stopped by a few times a week. He'd teach a little about one subject; food that was forbidden or combinations of foods that weren't permitted. Sometimes he would talk about the holiness of the 7th day- the day of rest- Shabbos.

I listened. I am sure I would have to hear the details many times before I could remember them.

I remembered bits and pieces of Shabbos; heavenly aroma of Challah and Mamme swaying by two candles. For now, others were feeding me and I didn't need to turn lights on and off, or try to prepare foods with those rules in mind. Nancy took care of all of this.

She was given a very general tutorial about the food re-warming. The Chabad community was graciously sending in lunch and dinners for us.

R'Berel would try to speak to Alex also. All falling under what a Chabad Rabbi did.

It seemed that in fact Alex Richards was Jewish. He was raised to never forget that. His grandfather passed away after his Bar Mitzva); grandfather Jules died of a heart attack, but in reality, he died slowly over years, from heart break! Relatives lost in the Holocaust. Close relatives. Alex's Babi Libby was taking this to heart even more and more. She was almost obsessed; for a long time trying to find out about survivors. Most neighbors and friends didn't return from whatever gehinom they had been taken! Only these two knew their shared guilt, Leba's more than her husband's though.

Challah {ceremonial bread}

Chabad {name of Chassidus which R'Berel represented}

Bar Mitzva {age 13 when boy becomes young man- obliged to fulfill Torah tenets}

Gehinom {purgatory}

Suddenly the clear English only spoken by this Richards clan, was not the only language his ears would hear. Yiddish and Rumanian/Hungarian-letters written, calls to Congressmen and Senators enlisting help with overseas Consulates

Calls to Rabbis; maybe they could find out about transports from Rumania environs, survivors and visas, out of Europe to anywhere remotely safer.

Shevios - his grandparents called it that- was a time they always lit yearly memorial candles. It seemed Babi had had a twin sister who was married with a houseful of children. From what they'd learned, the towns and cities were liquidated and transports to Auschwitz took place on Shevuos so they lit six candles each year. Tears and candles and regrets and recriminations. Never telling him what this was all about.

His Babi had always been youthful looking and in good shape; but she looked twenty years older since Poppa had passed away. Life insurance took care of the monetary worries; but she was like a waif, a lost soul and nothing his father Nate could do made much dent in the sadness. Nate was an only child as was his wife.

Shevuos {holiday seven weeks after Passover}

Babi {Grandmother}

Both had been raised to respect their elders and make sure they only married Jewish people. (It seemed discriminatory especially to his family that embraced all people and causes. It was taught to him as such; mothers determined whether a child was authentically Jewish. It had nothing to do with if a person was good; it was simply that to be authentically Jewish went only according to that inviolate rule of law).

His parents had even moved and taken an apartment on Babi Libby's block so they could take care of her needs, while she maintained some independent living.

In fact, Babi had told him that her Yiddish name was actually Leba; his Poppa's was Yehuda or Yidel as a nick name and his father Nate was actually Naftali. Obviously, Alex asked whether he too had a Hebrew name and was told, "Yes, you are named for a dear Abraham/Avrum." (This was the name of his biological father but he wouldn't know this until much later).

This was about all R'Berel would hear. He told Alex that many people from Rumania lit Yahr Zeit candles (memorial) candles) on Shevuos to commemorate the day the transports arrived at Auschwitz with most certain, extermination the same day.

Any further questions, could or should wait, he thought.

Yahrzeit candles {memorial candles}

The episode in Rumania about the twin sisters and the twin sons had been kept in the strictest confidence, actually within the walls of the Rebbe's residence, so at this moment, Berel didn't realize the significance of what Alex shared.

This would soon change because Nancy knew he'd been speaking to Alex. When the Gabbai in Cleveland made a call to Nurse Nancy she promptly told him, "Any questions about Alex would be best answered by either Alex himself or the Rabbi Berel; they've been talking and sharing."

The Gabbai told the Rebbe he would be speaking to R'Berel first to avoid asking any upsetting questions directly to Alex.

R'Berel knew the questions weren't idle and he answered all- one Rabbi to a greater one, with the knowledge that the information would be handled with utmost discretion.

Alex's parents were wealthy, living on the west coast, maybe Los Angeles and were very solicitous of their son. If he would relocate, they would visit the locale to be sure it would be a step "up" for him. He added that Nate's Hebrew name was Naftali, his grandmother's Hebrew name was Leba and his late grandfather was Yehuda, but known as Yidel. He Alex, was named after an Avrum.

This was important information. A plan had to be designed and implemented, so that Isaac and Nate didn't stumble upon each other without preparation.

If the Rebbe could be kept in the loop when Jack's affairs would be finalized and the move scheduled, would be important. Most likely, that would also be the time when Alex would come to check out Cleveland and make a decision for his own future.

There was very little time it seemed; Yaakov was eager to leave Skokie and join his Raizel and his newly found sister and family.

The challenge for the Rebbe and his wife; how to open this double pronged painful story effectively, and without damage?

There was no possibility when winter was approaching, that the Rebbe and Rebbetzin could contemplate making another trip, major or minor. They also could think of no acquaintances or connections that would know Mrs. Jules Richards.

The kindest way to cushion a possible blow, would be a letter. The Rebbetzin sat with the Rebbe to find the right words- not too much and not too little. It would either be met with interest or it would be ignored. What to do afterward, they could plan based on the outcome of the ad!

The letter was dictated to Sophie, as follows: (This after she and Isaac were given **some** details which bore similarity to the ad placed for a Jack/Yaakov Bekker/Baker). They would ask nothing and wait to be updated.

Confidential matter for Libby Richards and her son Nate:

I am R'Yosef, a Rebbe formerly from Rumania and now serving a community in Cleveland, Ohio. You, Mrs. Richards most likely would remember my brother," a/h" (may He rest in peace)– who served as the Rebbe in your town when you lived there. He was known throughout Europe, descendant of a holy Rabbinical dynasty.

At the time, twin sisters came to him with an unusual shaila.

Shaila {emotional question}

It was a challenging issue with many facets and in the end my brother, May He Rest in Peace, suggested options but gave no decision. One sister and husband remained in Rumania and suffered at the hands of Hitler (yemach shmoh v'zichro). The other sister was able to relocate to America. Contact between the two families ended once the trip to America was actualized.

I inherited this issue when my brother could no longer continue as a spiritual leader. I have important information concerning the Zilber family.

If you are interested in speaking with me, I can be reached via my Gabbai Shalom and here is the contact information (phone and address).

Please treat this letter with discretion, as I am, and will. Lives depend on this.

The letter sat in the drawer of the Rebbetzin's chest, for a few days. It was re-read to make sure it said enough, gently, but not too much. The Rebbe taking a young Yitzchak under his wing,

Yemach Shmoh V'Zichro {may his memory be obliterated}

did nothing to tarnish his opinion of his parents; he wouldn't be able to understand the pressure placed on them, by Leba and Yidel. If at any time, he was to join their family, it should be with the best potential for a wholesome upbringing. Their approach never changed; all for Yitzchak's good. Bitterness serves no one well. For now, the only ones that knew the entire history of Yitzchak and Naftuli was this saintly couple in Cleveland and Gabbai Shalom. Should they be contacted, the Rebbe would have to daven to know exactly how much of this to share, to whom and in what way. Perhaps Leba Reich (Richards in U.S.) would provide information that would inform the Rebbe's handling of this delicate matter!

Sophie and Isaac went to the post office to mail it, c/o Alex Richards in Skokie for either Mr. Nate Richards or Libby Richards. The envelope was marked "personal and confidential".

Now a very tense waiting time. The letter might take three or four business days to get to Alex and then another week to Libby or Nate; if he would in fact mail it or forward it promptly.

So best not to expect anything for ten days or so.

Gabbai Shalom was told that a very important call might come in for the Rebbe- either from Alex, someone called Nate or a woman named Libby, and

Daven {pray}

besides for prayers or Shabbos, the Rebbe was to be notified immediately in case of a return call or letter. The mail was picked up and processed promptly, to make sure nothing would be delayed or lost.

They couldn't wait to initiate the query; it was coinciding with Yaakov Bekker's move by ambulance. If this was the case it was possible Alex would miss the letter and they'd have to find another more secure and reliable method. Time was of the essence; they felt like they were racing against the clock.

Weather though delayed the ability to move Yaakov; ice and snow helped the Rebbe's mission. Alex did receive the letter, noted the inner envelope for his Babi or father and called his father. Nate told him, that he and his mother would be coming to Cleveland, the approximate arrival time and that Alex should be sure to bring this letter and give it over to him. Babi was staying home and if there was anything in the letter affecting her, Nate would update her.

So, it went. When weather conditions cooperated, Yaakov Bekker with Nancy and Alex was brought to his new apartment in Cleveland. Sophie and Isaac had gone all out, as had Iris. The place had been painted by Isaac and was homey with new beds, linens, towels and sets of dishes and pots. A ramp had been built for easier exit and access. A downstairs bedroom of sorts was cordoned off until Jack could safely manage the steps.

Jack settled in easily; his attitude was happy and hopeful.

Nancy would take another tutorial – this time from Sophie, based on the Rebbetzin's guidelines about how to warm and serve the food that would be provided by Iris, Sophie or take-out. She would be given a stipend if she wished to eat "out", but if yes, it had to be outside of the home. No unkosher foods could be brought into this home. Yaakov Bekker's food would be prepared and served k'halacha (according to Jewish dietary laws). Color coding helped identify dishes, flatware and pots as dairy, meat or pareve (neutral.

He was shown around and his welcoming committee-his granddaughter, Iris, Yechezkel, Ari, Moishi and Shana were on hand. Raizel looked happy to be reunited with her Poppa, Nancy and of course Alex.

Alex excused himself saying he would call a taxi and go to a hotel; his parents were arriving soon and they wanted to spend time with him. Normally, an offer to drive him would have been made. Here, no one wanted a chance meeting between Yitzchak and Alex's father Nate. No one wanted Alex to look at Yitzchak and recognize the similarities.

He also wanted to give Jack and his family, time to bond and re-connect. University or college options for him would be discussed; his parents would want to hear sound reasons for sudden changes

K'Halacha {according to Jewish law}

All agreed he would continue his studies for a higher degree and if relocating, he'd also need a place to live. His parents would want to be sure he was set up properly.

He had the letter in his pocket; he got the feeling its contents were life changing. He would hand it over, have a bite with his parents and then call it a night.

Of course, no one could ask or mention anything so the Rebbe and wife and Sophie were all quietly tense. Isaac felt the tension too.   Questions were never uttered. but the Rebbe handled so many problems; sometimes tension couldn't be avoided.

Tomorrow was a new day with much to accomplish. Alex would have to analyze where his future would be. His best approach always, in trying to make sound decisions was – plus and minus. He wouldn't know where he would put a leap of faith, was it a plus or a risky, minus, Raizel being the leap? He hadn't even dated her, only knowing her from the hospital, but she had become important to him.

When Alex arrives at the hotel, first thing he does is hug his father and mother, and then give him the envelope. His father puts it into his suit pocket and they proceed to have dinner and catch up. They decide on an itinerary for the next few days; not knowing it would change drastically though.

Before leaving, Alex reminds his father about the letter, which had already been forgotten.

Nate reads the letter, re-reads it and makes a call to his mother Libby. He first tells her that

Alex looks well and that he has stated sound reasons for wanting to relocate to Cleveland.

Then Nate tells his mother that Alex had met a grand Rabbi, one who came to minister to a Skokie family, but whose primary congregation was in Cleveland. He originated from Rumania. Nate could hear a palpable silence; Libby's undivided attention.

"Momma, I will read you the letter, I think it applies more to you than to me".

Libby listens to the brief message and sobs throughout. Thoughts about her sister Hinda, Avrum and family lost in the war were never far. She had never been able to understand why they didn't secure visas for the entire family; they had had the means. They hadn't written one letter, why in heavens name, hadn't they? Of course, no one could imagine, predict or internalize the devastation and death that one man could inflict on a continent's Yidden. Also, Leba recognized it would be difficult raising Naftali with any comments or questions from Hinda and Avrum. Distance back then had seemed like a good choice especially as Leba and Yidel morphed into Libby and Jules.

In her joy at having secured a Jewish child and fear - perhaps irrational-, she wanted to get away from her sister. In the beginning, she and Yidel meant to keep frum and keep their word about raising the child correctly. America with its opportunities and evident Anti-Semitism was the excuse they used and they slid, until they were only holding onto easy traditions.

Pain after the war, trying to locate her sister, brother in law or maybe any of the children was met with frustration. That no one from Rumania was looking for them either, was a painful reality. Totally forgetting that they'd Americanized their first and last names, making a search impossible, they put the past behind them. Hinda and Avrum would have had no way of knowing that many that came to America changed both their first and sur names, had they had the ability to contact the Reich family.

Libby wiping copious tears, asks that Nate call the telephone number for this Rabbi and to make a speaking appointment by phone. She would like to hear what this Rabbi wanted to say.

It is at this juncture that Isaac and Sophie hear the entire story and will anxiously await developments. Sophie sits close to Isaac, watching his every expression, ready to try to comfort or speak to him.

If ever he thought about his origins, he shut down, feeling as if he was betraying the only parents, he knew- this Rebbe and Rebbetzin. They will assure him now, that he has a right to his blood mishpucha.

All know this will affect Alex, his parents and this Libby Richards. Everyone's world will be upended with these truths.

Frum {religiously observant}

Up to now, Nate knew he was an only child. Libby would wait to hear what the Rebbe wishes to share; she was sure finally making things right, would be made clear to her. It was time for her to honor some semblance of her promise to her sister Hinda, long overdue, actually!

One request, one decision; one act that is put into motion and it can and does spiral out in unforeseen directions. Once out of one's hands, it is also out of one's control. Libby tries to formulate an introduction to a very painful conversation and truth. To have kept this a secret for decades has been a very heavy burden.

Libby will join her family in Cleveland. This can't be handled effectively via phone.

Nate meets his "mother" Libby and realizes that her coming to Cleveland has very little to do with seeing where Alex may continue his career and life. She's distracted and seems to have aged dramatically since he saw her a few days ago. Her usual elegant grooming and outfit are not in evidence, and this more than anything is the proof that something is awfully wrong.

He checks her accommodation and asks whether she would like tea or coffee; he will order coffee for himself. Perhaps she needs to see a doctor? She says all she does need is a hot cup of strong and sweet coffee and G-d's help; and once it arrives and she's holding the china cup, she begins.

"Nate, I have something very painful to tell you. Her mentioning of G-d was a give-away that something serious was afoot. She rarely brought Gd into any conversation. That would change though! "I wish your Poppa was here to help me explain. Truth, if I wasn't confronted with no way out, I'd leave things as they've been. That

is because as much as I have loved you, I have been very cowardly and selfish."

Nate tries to interrupt her, but Libby quiets him. "Let me speak, please! You know how hard Poppa and I tried to find my family after the atrocities of the Holocaust were made evident. To have twin sisters separated so brutally is something I can't describe and yet I have done the same thing- twin siblings were separated primarily because of me. My sister had a large family and I hadn't had children in about ten years of marriage; it didn't look hopeful. Hinda, my sister/best friend was again in the family way and I don't know where I got the chutzpa, the nerve to even ask if I could take the infant and raise it as my own. Once I said it once, I was able to keep asking and it was creating a wedge between us, two, who had been like one. How could I even imagine what I was asking, that a mother give her child away- I who had none couldn't know how very much I was demanding.

"When she gave birth to twin boys, it was like a **sign** to me, it was right; one for her and one for me. She didn't want to, but I was determined, actually obsessed, would be the better word. This was my chance and my husband's chance to be parents. We would be able to give the child much, much more than they could. Who knew what the future held for the Jews in all the European cities and towns? I suggested we put the question to our Rebbe and we'd both abide by his decision. This Rebbe, so great, was troubled by the question. When he answered, it was not with a decision, but with options.

"One condition though was inviolate; the child was to be raised to follow the tenets of the Torah. We agreed and my sister and her husband, Hinda and

Avrum, reluctantly handed over Naftali to us. Yitzchak remained with them."

Libby has to stop, because Nate is asking her what she means; what is she saying?

Libby repeats: "I am telling you that you Nate, Yiddish name Naftuli had a twin brother Yitzchak and the biological parents were Hinda and Avrum Zilber; my sister and brother in law- may they rest in peace!"

She must continue or she won't be able to. "We were ecstatic and showering our Naftuli with love, that had waited and accumulated for ten years. Freedoms in our town were tightening and Yidel, thought it best for us to secure visas and try to leave, while we still could. Why didn't we use our money to secure visas for my sister, husband and her children; I don't know. All I know is we left and they remained in Europe, to suffer the pain, the anxiety, the persecutions, the deprivations and the ultimate deaths, six among the myriad millions.

"America didn't want the public to know the extent of the atrocities; coverage in the media was back burner if at all. U.S. entered the war because of the attack on Pearl Harbor. Had that not happened, the Allies would have consisted of countries without U.S. Only after the war, when survivors began speaking did we begin to understand the extent of destruction. Many didn't wish to speak; information and details only trickled out.

"We did try to find our families; to no avail. We believed there had been no Zilber survivors.

"Life in U.S. - this "goldine medina" - wasn't as welcoming as one would think. Jews bring their brains, their brawn, their ethics and contribute and build up a country; just as we have done for thousands of years in all our other exiles. Yet the discrimination was there. We decided to become Libby and Jules Richards, Americanizing the Reich sur name, and your first name to become Nate. We thought this might ensure more acceptance and less discrimination. Once no one had survived; you were our son and we thought the journey to our parenthood would never come to light."

Nate asks, "So what has changed now? Why after all this time, do you feel the need to upend my entire understanding of who I am and who my parents are and aren't?"

Libby answers, "This is the easiest part of this conversation. My Rebbe's brother took over being the Rebbe and he moved to Cleveland post war. He was needed to help a family in Skokie and totally out of the regular protocol, this Rebbe asked his foster son- Isaac/Yitzchak and wife Sophie to accompany him and his Rebbetzin on that particular mission. This Sophie saw Alex and Alex so resembles you; it's impossible not to notice and put the pieces together. Pictures of a young Yitzchak more starkly proved this. Sophie wouldn't give up on this similarity. The Rebbe and Rebbetzin had no choice but to try to find out who Alex belonged to, for this reason and possibly others."

Nate runs his hands through his hair and says, "I would like to meet my twin Isaac and this Rebbe. Does Isaac know?"

Libby answers that the Rebbe said he would first speak to Yitzchak- to prepare him, and then Libby would have the conversation with Naftuli. Yitzchak will be at the Rebbe's home, which is his home as well, and they will be given a private room for this sensitive meeting, rather than his suite on the third floor. His wife Sophie will be there for him and with him, when you call that you wish to meet.

"No one could have foreseen that we'd feel the need to move away. Neither of us would have predicted that we would slowly break our word and not keep the mitzvos which were our life. It wasn't one act or a single conscious decision, it was an erosion over time. No one could have envisioned that the entire Europe would be plundered, burned and destroyed.

"Perhaps one bright side was that Hinda's two twins survived, albeit in different ways. He was given to people, that would hide him until the end of the war; he was then raised as this Rabbi's child. You were nurtured and raised by de facto parents, albeit blood relatives who have loved you.

"I hope in time you will be able to forgive me. I hope my sister and brother in law in Heaven and Yitzchak here and now, L'havdil, will be able to forgive me at some point. I am the only one left to accept responsibility. I don't believe I will ever forgive myself.

Mitzvos {torah tenets}

L'Havdil {to separate the departed from the living}

What I might be able to do, one small thing, is to give Yitzchak an idea of what his mother would look like today. Next time I am here, or any time, if he wishes to receive me, I will also bring the few photographs, I've kept all these years. It's a small thing compared to the "avla" I committed. It was me. I put my husband up to it."

Avla {egregious ill}

The Rebbe and Rebbetzin were in attendance to greet Nate Richards. Sophie in her inimical way, had put out hot drinks, cookies, soft drinks and some fruit.

Isaac and Nate met and stood looking at each other- same face, hair, build; with totally different experiences and outlooks on life. Yitzchak had been fortunate to be nurtured by this great Rabbinical family and was a keeper of his parents' faith. Naftali had been robbed of truth, of the cream of his heritage, and now was feeling the pain of being orphaned; but also feeling betrayed and mislead. In time he would be able to embrace the blessing of a twin and find joy in the relationship. Recapturing a lost heritage, another journey. Accepting that his life was built on untruths, seemed out of reach now. Perhaps he would need a Rabbinical advisor or counseling, to be to heal and try to forgive. His wife Anna was with him and would be with him, in this every step of the way.

They would talk hours that night, the next day and over the next weeks and months; never to lose touch again.

Nate also wanted to connect with the Rebbe; hear about his parents and his brother, the past Rebbe, that was involved in that fateful decision. Nate would grapple with the differences between an observant twin brother and the suave sophistication that wealth and good education had brought him. A brother who was victimized in Europe as compared to a sheltered existence in America. Was there any way to bridge the two?

The Rebbe spoke to Naftuli, as he called him, and his wife and told him there were many ways every day to serve Hashem; one would be to continue to respect the woman who raised him. Anger was a corrosive emotion and it bred more anger and negative impulses. He should live as we all live, taking everything step by step and day by day. He could take on "mitzvos" slowly should he wish to; and receive guidance in the order of priority of that journey. Each was wrapped with beautiful history and meaning!   Also, there was no need for him to make any changes in name; in Hebrew he was correctly Naftali ben (son of) Hinda or ben Avraham, {Hebrew identification of children son or daughter of either mother's first name during life or at passing, father's first name}.

The Rebbe's brother had known both Hinda and Leba as well as their husbands. If Hinda Zilber trusted Leba, then she would want her Naftuli to strive to embrace the truth and make the best of the reality. The pain would subside and to give time, its own time, for healing and understanding.

One thing he could and should do though, was to study "kaddish" so he could recite it for his parents.

Kaddish (prayer said for deceased)

Yizkor next! Another important mitzva was the donning of tefillin. This was a commandment on all young men from the age of thirteen/Bar Mitzva. He would be taught method and provided with a pair, if/ when he was ready to follow through. (The Rebbe was thinking about Yaakov who had also been introduced to this mitzva by R'Berel. He though would need help physically to don them daily, when he indicated his readiness to follow through).

The Rebbe was hopeful that in time, Naftuli would begin to learn and accept the mitzvos.

Leba Richards could paint a picture of Yitzchak's parents for him; when he was able and/or ready to speak with her. He had no memories of anything but this saintly Rebbe and Rebbetzin. They had tried to give him a notion of life in Europe and his parents but Leba could do it more fully and vividly. She had some old formal pictures; the twins at several stages, the two chasunas and one with Yidel, Hinda and the family pre-twins. Their meetings, not immediate, were painful and awkward but necessary for Isaac to find closure. Sophie in turn shared the few pictures she had of Isaac, the catalyst for this family's reuniting.

Yizkor (prayer for deceased recited on specific holiday)

Mitzva (commandment)

Tefillin (Phylacteries)

Chasunas (weddings)

Isaac and Nate had many questions. It was left to
the Rebbe and Rebbetzin to answer them, in the
gentlest way. His grandmother-Babi / aunt, and
father/mother would stand in the background. The
aim was that there be acceptance, peace without
rancor or blame.

It would be up to Alex, how he would proceed with
his Babi Libby. In the end, he followed his
parents' lead. Things were strained in the
beginning and then slow healing set in, at its own
pace. He was young, hopeful to build his life and
ready to follow Raizel's model and include new
people as family.

One could think they were managing their feelings
well, and then there would be a set-back of anger
or misunderstanding.

Pressure in this matter would just damage the
fragile beginnings. This Rabbi and his wife would
be ready, whenever needed to help iron issues out.
They reiterated, slow healing and forgiveness was
the only viable path.

Raizel Baker proved to be a great support to Alex.
Her world had very recently changed dramatically
with the arrival of the Levy family. Left out of
her narrative was the mirror, the woman and the
catalyst for Levy's searching for a Yaakov Bekker,
per the Rebbe's direction and guidance.

She focused on what she had; an uncle, an aunt,
cousins- a family to share good times with and the
more challenging. She was part of a FAMILY for a
very long time in her life! She encouraged Alex
to be open to embracing new relationships and
directions in life. He would be the richer, as
she was enriched. A huge bonus was the Rebbe and

Rebbetzin, who embodied unconditional devotion, steadfastness and trustworthy models of goodness.

She'd remind him that no one could even imagine or judge how threats and victimization in cruel gentile regimes impacted on Jewish families. Desperate times brought out desperation in people. Certainly, it seemed each tried to do their very best. Not she and not Alex, could know how they would react in similar circumstances. Her wish, no one should ever be tested in this way!

Raizel shared this all with me, her new cousin and confidante. I was happy for her; doubts about Alex's lineage now wouldn't stand in their way if they would in fact court and marry. She referred to this entire saga as a mystical journey.

I could only share this journey within family, when I needed to revisit it, and Raizel was definitely that. My friends would ask many questions; what could Skokie possibly offer for the entire summer vacation. Would we return for the upcoming summer? My answers followed my mother's approach. To my closest friends I confidently said that my parents had wanted to take us on a mystical journey and they nodded, like they understood what that was. Me, I am still taking it in.

It's I guess it's fitting for me, Shana, to finish this saga as I was the one who Bubba Bluma sought out. We will never know why she reached out to me, if I was the first one or only one to react. The Rebbetzin explained this to me. I do know that I haven't seen her since. I hope that means she is finally resting in peace; she so deserves that! The sketches and Yaakov's memories are all we have by way of a picture of her. Her influence though lives on in us all. I was mistaken though-had I been near my mirror, I would have seen her reflection with its first smile. I would be her last stop; none of us ever saw her since!

My parents and Raizel encouraged me to focus on eighth grade and enjoy the milestones of graduation, class trip and beginning High School. She told me it would fly by, hers did, and I should put the mirror, the visits, the messages out of my head.

They would always remain in my heart, as this experience was life altering. So maybe I do know what a mystical journey is.

All I can say is something I heard Sophie repeat from the Rebbe while He was preparing the trip to Cleveland: **"A Maaseh mit ah Shpigel"**.

I asked her what it meant, as I couldn't ask my Mother who didn't know Yiddish and I wouldn't disturb a Rebbetzin with this question. She said that sometimes something happens and it becomes very complicated; in Yiddish people would refer to that as a "Maaseh mit ah ___". I got it then. The image in the mirror sending seeming mystical messages, causing our family to become acquainted with a holy person, for direction and clarity. Bubba Bluma put in motion the reunification of not only her own children but also another family that needed to know each other, and make good on past mistakes.

It's almost as if her insistent visits, brought elements together, like Bekker braided Challah.

As I write this, we have become one large extended family and like all families, there are weaker links at unexpected times, that hopefully will be healed, over time. Leba who has bought a small house in Cleveland is a bridge to our understanding of life in pre-war Europe and post war America. Slowly she's returning to her roots. She visits with Alex and Yaakov and my Mom; Yaakov especially likes to hear her speak Yiddish which reminds him of his beloved Mamme. We refer to Isaac and Sophie as Uncle and Tanta; honorary titles. My Uncle Yaakov is frail but loves to spend time with his sister Iris, Zeke as he calls my father as he can't pronounce his full name- Yechezkel- easily. Ari and Moishi though are clearly his favorites. Somehow when they are reviewing their Hebrew lessons, he and Alex appear and sit nearby, trying to also absorb some of the information. Sometimes on Friday afternoons, one of them plays "teacher" with Jack and Alex as students.   Nate and his wife spend time here more and more, and when in Cleveland, he's never without his twin brother, helping in any way the Rebbe's household requires.

I am watching up close what living a life of faith actually is and have been given a bird's eye view of what life in Europe, pre- war, with Rebbe guidance was and might have grown into. Europe, especially Poland was the seat of Chassidus and a pinnacle level of piety and learning!

This saintly couple healed many raw wounds and much pain- slowly and gently, like nursing a bird with a broken wing back to strong and full functionality. They gave Uncle Yaakov "chiyus". My parents were rewarded with family and the truth about my Mother's history. Uncle Isaac has his twin Nate; will live to honor their deceased parents.

Forgiveness, devotion and appreciation are ingredients that both enrich our families. What is most surprising to me though is, how unassuming and humble this Grand Rabbi and his special Rebbetzin were and are, as they bonded the new roots of our fragile and very precious families and heritage.

Chiyus {emotional vitality}

If I didn't know of their greatness, I'd think they were like anyone's Babi and Zaidi!

We Levy's now have a full table for each Shabbos and Yom Tov- that is when we aren't invited to the Rebbe's personal "tisch" (table), as family!

What I can take forever from this unforgettable experience is that life isn't a fairy tale. Adults aren't in control the way their children imagine they are. They make tough decisions -not black and white but gray- while making things look and feel easy. Even deciding to confer with a Rebbe, rather than take action alone was an important lesson, going forward. Adult life also doesn't guarantee an upward trajectory in any fashion- (I looked this word up). One has to persevere though, no matter what.

I have witnessed my Uncle Yaakov have to fight to re-learn basic life skills, i.e. simple speech and walking. I've met Libby who had to very humbly own painful and expensive behavior that hurt her sister/brother in law and ultimately the son she raised. She could have run from it or not face it, and if so, would have been the biggest loser, constantly carrying the burden of her misdeed. My cousin Raizel, so young and with so much heart break and loss, able to face a fresh new beginning with hope. I've learned up front about The Cantonist era and Holocaust - the Rebbe and Rebbetzin bear the tattooed numbers to prove excruciatingly painful memories upon which they too rebuilt a rewarding life.

Babi and Zaidi {Grandmother & Grandfather}

A woman- Nancy-from another culture, ready to respect and courageously invest in our broken family, and become a part of our family, is another source of inspiration.

No matter which person or aspect of this story, I see faith, persistence and patience. I am grateful- my mother has a new peace, no questions, no doubts; the missing pieces located and fit. I only realize this now since she has found her origins and knows why she was given up for adoption.

We all, this very extended family are the richer for this mystical journey.

The End but really the beginnings for many!

Made in the USA
San Bernardino, CA
19 April 2020